# *A* HOME *for* HOPE

KIMBERLY SPRAYBERRY

ISBN 978-1-63844-433-6 (paperback)
ISBN 978-1-63844-434-3 (digital)

Christian Faith Publishing, Inc.
832 Park Avenue
Meadville, PA 16335
www.christianfaithpublishing.com

Printed in the United States of America

Thank you to Karley Conklin for all of your help and guidance. A special thank you to my family, especially my amazing husband Doug for your love and support on this journey. God bless each of you.

# CHAPTER 1

The distinctive church spires of the Holy City gradually rose into view as the *USS America* gently eased into the Charleston Harbor on a late-July evening. Excitement echoed throughout the berthing compartments of the naval aircraft carrier as the sailors shuffled about, preparing to dock at the Charleston Naval Shipyard in South Carolina after an eight-month deployment conducting missions for NATO in the Mediterranean.

Steve Parnell, after serving nine years in the Navy and spending nearly a year on this latest mission, was more than ready to be off this ship and had finished packing the last of his belongings into his duffle bag hours ago. Wanting to be alone with his thoughts, he quickly inched his way up the labyrinth of floors and narrow stairwells leading to the flight deck. As he walked past the darken windows of one of the three wardrooms where he had so many meals with his shipmates, he noticed his reflection in the glass, and he stopped to gaze at the man he saw. Looking back was a strong tall twenty-six-year-old man sporting the standard crew-cut hairstyle of those in the armed forces. Before enlisting, Steve liked to wear his black hair longer, but it usually took some taming due to the unruliness of its natural curl. He wasn't sure he liked what he saw. Sure, on the outside he was handsome and fit, but it was what's behind his sky-blue eyes that troubled him. He didn't have time to mull over that now. He was ready to be off this ship and onto dry land.

A few moments later, as Steve made his way up to the main deck, he took a deep breath, inhaling the familiar coastal breeze tinged with puff mud and sweet grass. He looked out longingly toward the familiar French Quarter and Downtown District. He was returning home with a heavy heart for several reasons. He felt more than a little guilty to be alive and safely home when so many young men drafted into the Vietnam War, which had just ended three months earlier, weren't so lucky. America lost 58,000 men and had over 150,000 injured. Some survivors lost limbs and were maimed for life.

The Navy alone lost over 1,600 men and more than 4,000 were wounded. Steve enlisted before the war started and was never on the ground in Vietnam but had been stationed in Southeast Asia for several years as the Navy provided the allied effort and projection of the US combat power ashore while assuming control of the surrounding seas. Sadly, those troops who did return weren't getting the *hero's welcome* they deserved. They were labeled "baby killers" by many at home perpetuated weekly by the negative news broadcasts.

Westward, the sun painted the sky with streaks of pink, yellow, and orange as it slipped silently into the choppy waves of the Ashley River. *If you listen hard enough, you can hear the water sizzle*, Steve's grandmother had told him so many years ago as they'd watched the sun making its daily descent as they strolled together along the high battery near White Point Garden. *How many sunsets like this did we share when I was younger?* Steve wondered. Charleston was one of his grandmother's favorite cities on earth, and they vacationed there each summer, as a family, for a long as he could remember. Steve could clearly see his grandmother's sweet smile gazing down at him as a boy, her beautiful face lit by the warm glow of the sun, but that happy thought was quickly replaced by the memory of the last time he saw his grandmother and the pain in her eyes. Steve shook his head and recoiled inwardly, hating himself and knowing he was the one who put it there.

Sighing deeply, Steve looked out longingly over the familiar French Quarter and Downtown District, trying to erase his painful memories, too many to recount. *I need a drink*, he thought to himself. *I wonder if The Brick on Fulton Street is serving drinks yet?* Before he enlisted, Steve spent several nights in the popular nightclub when he turned eighteen and could legally purchase beer but not liquor. That would be his first stop tonight as soon as they docked.

As the ship finally passed under the Grace Memorial and Pearman Bridges on its final leg up Cooper River, he was startled by a deep and quite familiar voice intruding welcomingly into his troubled thoughts.

"Lieutenant Parnell?"

"Yes, sir," he answered as he turned and saluted his approaching commander.

"Before we dock, I just want to commend you for a job well done. You're a well-respected leader among your men," the commander said as he raised his hand to return the lieutenant's salute. "You have done an excellent job with your men while at sea, especially during the attack a few weeks ago. You may not realize it, but your bravery saved many lives that day. You've earned some well-deserved R & R. Do you think you'll reenlist, or are you going to retire?"

"I don't know, sir. I have some personal things I need to take care of at home."

"Got a girl waiting on you?" the commander asked with a jovial smile while bumping him lightly and intentionally with his shoulder.

"No, sir! Not yet." Steve said reluctantly smiling and looking away.

The commander shook his head. "I hope you'll consider coming back. I'm sure there'll be a promotion to commander waiting on you. If you don't return, it'll definitely be the Navy's loss, but I understand. You're still young and need to take time to figure out what it is you want out of life and what'll make you happy."

"I'll give it some thought, sir," Steve said as he picked up and stowed his duffle bag in an out-of-the-way place to help ready the ship for docking.

"Well, have a great time in town. I hope to see you again soon," the commander said, shaking Steve's hand.

"Thank you, sir," Steve replied as the commander turned and walked away. *You wouldn't think so highly of me if you really knew me.*

His thoughts returned to his grandmother and all the horrible things he said the night he left.

With hundreds of sailors now up on all decks, there were still jobs to be done getting the ship safely moored to the pier as instructions and demands were being thrown in all different directions. If everyone didn't pull their weight and pay attention, men could easily be injured. Immediate repairs were needed to fix a broken engine coupling before the ship's eventual return to its port city of Norfolk, Virginia. Everyone was leaving the ship for a few days, and those who lived in South Carolina could go home instead of having to back track from Virginia unnecessarily.

With his job done and mission complete, it was finally time for Steve to head toward the ramp, preparing to disembark. *Disembark to where? Will Granny let me come home after the way I've hurt her? It's so ironic.* He'd become a man whom others respected, and he did it all without the help of her Jesus, *their* Jesus, thinking momentarily of his long-lost and beloved parents. *I can't believe I stayed away for nine years without a single letter or call to let her know I was okay, except for the one-and-only postcard I sent her to let her know I had enlisted and hadn't died when I left home. Is enlisted the same thing as running away? It sure felt like it. Will she be proud of me, though, after all I've accomplished, or is our relationship damaged forever?*

After taking a cab to and visiting *The Brick* for a couple of drinks, Steve began his search on foot for a room for the night. As he exited the noisy bar, the evening was warm, and a gentle breeze blew as Steve meandered down the uneven sidewalks, looking for a place to stay. Completely exhausted, Steve checked in to the first place he found, Fulton Lane Inn. Since being stuck on a ship for nearly a year and sharing a claustrophobia-inducing bunk with a crazy, Jesus-freak bunkmate, he was looking forward to some well-deserved time alone on a double bed where he planned to stretch out completely and sleep for the next several hours. Tomorrow he would think about his grandmother and heading home to Greenville, South Carolina. *Maybe.*

*****

Darcy Collins knew without a doubt her husband, Dillon, wouldn't forget their special plans tonight. She only worried his work would get in the way, like it so often did. *God, please let him come home on time tonight,* she prayed, then hurried around the kitchen, putting the finishing touches on his favorite meal—steak and shrimp, baked potatoes, and salad for their first-year anniversary. Just as she placed their favorite rolls in the oven, Darcy heard the front door open. Wiping her hands and rushing from the kitchen to quickly check her appearance in the hall mirror before heading around the corner into the living room hoping for the happy anniversary hug and kiss she imagined all day, but instead she arrived just in time to see Dillon drop his medical bag in front of the hall table by the door and then slowly make his way to the sofa and collapse in a tired heap. He immediately laid his head against the overstuffed blonde suede pillows, which caused his curly black hair to appear even darker, and he closed his eyes, never making eye contact with Darcy.

"Hey, sweetheart," Darcy said as she hurried to the sofa and sat beside her husband, placing her arms around him to welcome him home. He responded with a half hug with his left arm, but no kiss followed. Darcy's heart sank. So far this wasn't going the way she'd planned at all.

Trying to keep things light, she said, "Happy anniversary, Dillon. Dinner is almost ready. I'm making all of your favorites. Isn't it hard to believe today is here already? It seems like just yesterday we were standing before Pastor Watson as he performed the ceremony."

Dillon only nodded and sighed while leaning forward on both arms putting his head in his hands, raking his fingers through his already unruly hair.

Not knowing how to comfort him and rouse him from his obvious stupor, Darcy said, "Oh honey, I'm sorry. Here I am rattling on and haven't given you two seconds to say anything."

"I'm sorry, Darcy. Happy anniversary, sweetheart. I'm just so tired. Today's been one of the most stressful days at the office in a long time."

"Darling, why don't you wash up and just relax while I put dinner on the table. Then you can tell me all about your day." She slowly stood and leaned over him. She kissed his forehead as she touched his cheek with her hand. He smiled up at her, making eye contact for the first time since arriving home. She then headed toward the kitchen to keep an eye on the rolls.

A few minutes later, Darcy called to Dillon who was washing his hands in the bathroom. "Dinner's ready, sweetheart." Darcy could hear the water running and being turned off as she sat down alone at the dining room table. Dillon soon joined her.

"Everything looks great. I'm starving," he said as they joined hands and Dillon prayed for their meal. "Dear Lord, thank you for salvation and for blessing us so much. Thank you for our home and my successful career. Thank you, especially, for Darcy and our first year together. Thank you for this wonderful meal she's prepared. Bless this food to the nourishment of our bodies. Help us to grow closer to you, Lord, and to live by your example. Help us be loving and forgiving, and give us the wisdom to know when to give others grace as you have given to us so freely. Amen." Before they let go of each other's hands, Dillon squeezed Darcy's hands three times, which was their special silent signal meaning *I love you*. Dropping hands, they quickly dove into the meal before them.

"I'm so glad you made it home tonight in time for dinner," she said as she offered him the plate of rolls.

Taking one and setting it down on the edge of his own full plate, he said, "Darling, it's only by the grace of God I did make it home on time. I really should've stayed. There was still so much to do, but I knew how important tonight is to you, and I want you to know you're more important to me than anything. Today was terribly busy." He smoothed his hands over the napkin in his lap. "Of course, I had my usual rounds at the hospital and then all the paperwork at the office. Just as I was closing up, I received an emergency call."

"Oh, no. What happened?"

"It was a car wreck. A man was killed, and a little girl was injured."

"Oh, Dillon. I'm so sorry, sweetheart. Was it anyone we know?"

"No. The little girl was hysterical, screaming something about *'don't let my daddy leave me too.'* I think the pediatric doctor finally gave her something to calm her down so they could examine her for injuries."

"That poor little girl. How old is she?"

"She looked to be six or seven."

"Does she know about her father?"

"I don't know. She was sleeping when I left. The department of social services is trying to locate her next of kin."

"Oh, honey, I'm sorry. I can't imagine how hard that is on you. After dinner, why don't I run you a hot bath and bring you a glass of wine so you can relax and let the day's worries soak away. I'll clean up the kitchen, and then we can snuggle in bed and maybe watch TV. I think *Hollywood Squares* is on tonight," she said as she peered into his cobalt-blue eyes, which were heavy with worry and fatigue.

"That sounds wonderful, honey. Are you sure you won't be hurt if we don't go out for drinks and dancing tonight?"

"No, not at all," she said, looking slowly down at her knee-length flared-sleeve polyester green-and-yellow paisley dress and platform shoes. "I knew when I married a doctor there would be times when our plans would have to wait. Plus, I can see how tired you are."

"I know, but tonight is a very special night, and I don't want you to think you aren't the most important person in the world to me."

"I know how much you love me, baby. We can celebrate out on the town later. Besides, I think I'm ovulating," she said, looking Dillon square in the eyes as a blush colored her cheeks. "It might be better to stay in anyway and we can get a head start on our own festivities," she said playfully.

He stared at her in silence as if he were piecing together what she had just said. A broad smile finally grew across his face, showing his beautiful white teeth. Then he quickly stood, pulling her up with him. He kissed her quickly with the love and passion Darcy had been waiting for all day. When he finally pulled away breathlessly, he said while kissing her forehead, "You're so wonderful. Most wives would be angry if their husband didn't take them out on their anniversary. How about after my bath, we take advantage of you ovulating?" After a quite pause, Dillon tilted his head, playfully narrowed his eyes at his wife, and said, "Wait a minute, weren't you just ovulating a couple of weeks ago?"

She stared at him and grinned. "Well?" she said in a coy voice. "That was last month, and besides, you can't question Mother Nature."

They both chuckled, sitting back down to finish their meal. Darcy grabbed his hand and squeezed. She smiled as their eyes met. She could hardly wait for dinner to be over and their romantic evening to begin.

"Happy anniversary," she whispered before placing another bite in her mouth.

"So how was your day? Were you able to bake the cakes for the bake sale tomorrow at the church?"

*That stupid bake sale.* "No, I didn't get them finished, but it shouldn't take me long. I'll have them ready tomorrow."

Once their meal was complete, Darcy rose to clear the table. "I have a surprise for you, your favorite dessert."

"No, you didn't. White chocolate mousse cake?" Dillon asked, groaning. "Dinner was so delicious, honey. I'm not sure I could eat another bite."

Nodding and smiling, she said, "Don't be silly. I'll just cut you a tiny piece for now, and the coffee is already made." I'll take the dishes to the sink and be right back with both." She stood, grabbing the plates as she went toward the kitchen when the phone rang. "Don't answer it, honey. Just let it ring."

"You know I can't do that," Dillon said, walking toward the rotary phone on the long lampstand in the hallway. "Hello? Yes, this is Dillon. Slow down, I can't understand you."

Returning from the kitchen quickly, Darcy placed the dessert and coffee on the coffee table and joined Dillon in the hallway. "Who is it?" she mouthed.

Dillon held his hand up to stop her questions. "Cindy, calm down. I can hardly understand what you're saying."

Darcy crossed into the living room and plunked down on the sofa and crossed her arms in frustration, waiting for him to hang up. Huffing and rolling her eyes knowingly, she thought, *He better not leave me tonight. Doctor or no doctor, he better not leave me alone on our anniversary. Someone else can go in for a change.*

"How badly are you hurt?" he asked the female voice on the other line. "Are you bleeding? Where's Michael right now?" Even more curious now, Darcy walked straight back to Dillon's side.

"Look, Cindy, I've done all I know to do. You do realize he's not going to stop hitting you until he gives up drinking or you leave him, or you end up dead. Please. Please, just call the police this time," he pled with her. Darcy could hear the muffled high-pitched voice coming from the phone as Dillon continued to listen. "I know you are scared, but it's the only choice. Do you want me to call the police for you?"

Darcy clearly heard Cindy frantically yell, "No, Dillon! Don't!" And then she heard an uncontrollable sobbing. "Okay, okay. Cindy, just stop crying. I'll be there in a few minutes," he said as he quickly hung up the phone. He turned to face Darcy who was standing mere inches away, glaring up at him.

"Cindy who?" she snapped. "You can't be serious? What's happened that's so important you have to leave me on our anniversary?"

"Cindy Parnell Hogan. She's originally from Greenville. Remember, I told you about her a couple of times. She and her husband Michael live on Ashley Avenue?" He tried to console her. "Honey, please try to understand."

"Don't 'honey' me!" she yelled, her brows knitted tight and her teeth clenched. "Let someone else go to her."

"I can't. Cindy's one of my patients, and we went to school together as children. I've known her family forever. She's in an abusive marriage and needs help. She's terrified to call the police or leave. Her husband's been drinking and has beaten her again."

"Again? If she's so stupid to stay in the relationship, why is it your problem to take care of her now that she's hurt? Why can't she just go to the hospital or call someone else?"

"She's afraid the police will lock him up if she goes to the hospital and then he'll take it out on her even more when he comes home. I'm the only one she trusts right now," he tried to explain, closing his eyes and taking a deep breath and slowly exhaling.

"Then just go! Take care of your precious friend! I hope she's worth it!" Darcy yelled with tears brimming unnoticed in her eyes.

"What's that supposed to mean?" he shouted as she stormed away toward the door. Dillon reached down to pick up his doctor bag, and he turned and looked a last time at Darcy before leaving. "It's my job. You know that."

"Yeah, go ahead and leave. I'm sure she's more important to you than me or our anniversary." He heard Darcy say as he slammed the door and hurried toward his light-blue 1972 Volkswagen Beetle convertible parked in the driveway.

Darcy ran immediately toward their bedroom and flung herself onto the bed. Tears began flowing down her sullen face and red cheeks. *I can't believe he would leave me on our first anniversary, especially for another woman,* she thought to herself. She knew she was being irrational, but feelings of anger and disappointment overcame her. She sat up looking around for something to hit or throw. She forcefully threw her feather pillow across the room and collapsed again onto the bed. She cried until sleep slowly overcame her and taking her into a world of darkness and restless sleep.

*****

Slowing rolling onto his back for about the millionth time since lying down on the too-soft bed of the inn, Steve stared at the ceiling. He missed the gentle sway of the ocean to lull him to sleep. He missed the familiar clinking of metal sounds of his naval ship at night and the various snores of his shipmates. Huffing in exasperation, *it's too quiet to sleep*, he thought, rolling over on his side this time. Being stateside again and this close to home, he finally let himself admit he missed something and someone else. He missed home and his loving grandmother. He missed the way things used to be before he left.

*I can't believe it's been nine years since I've seen or talked to Granny,* he reflected as the horrible argument with his grandmother played over and over in his mind. Once the memories started, he couldn't make them stop. Knowing sleep was a battle he wouldn't win tonight, he rose from the bed and began pacing around the room with nervous energy. He walked over to his duffle bag and began stowing his naval uniforms in the tiny closet. *I should have thought to hang them up when I first got here. They will be wrinkled,* he silently chastised himself.

Turning back toward the bed, he noticed the red lights on the clock glowed a bright 1:57 a.m. *What are you still doing up? Why can't you just go to sleep? You must get some rest. You have a lot to do in the next few days,* he thought as he returned to the still-warm bed to try to sleep once again. He stretched his muscular six-foot body across the bed and pulled the sheet and covers up to his chin. Exhaustion finally claimed him as he drifted into a restless, dream-filled sleep.

# CHAPTER 2

Steve Parnell stretched his muscular arms above his head as he woke. Rising from the bed, he stumbled to the shower. He knew he wouldn't be able to enjoy his newfound freedom from Navy life until he called his grandmother to see if she would speak to him after all he had done. He showered and dressed and walked back to the bed. Once seated on the foot of the bed, he stared at the phone, minutes slowly ticking past. He knew what needed to be done, but he was unable to force his trembling hands to pick up the receiver and dial the number he swore he'd never dial again. *What if she won't talk to me? What if she never forgives me? What if...* question after question ran through his mind giving him many excuses not to place the call. *I'll call her this afternoon after I've had time to think about what I want to say.* He rose abruptly, walked out the door and closed it harder than he intended to. *Shoot!* he chided himself. *I can't believe I locked the keys in the room. Well, I'll have to get the front desk to let me in when I return.*

*****

Startled from a sound sleep by the steady banging on the door, Darcy bolted from bed, trying to comprehend what was going on. *Where's Dillon?* she thought as she wrapped the silk bathrobe around her body and saw her precious husband had not returned from his

visit to Cindy's house. She hurried to the door as the banging continued. "Hold on, I'm coming," she yelled. Her heart was pounding and
hands shaking as she debated on opening the door since her husband
wasn't there.

"Who is it?" she yelled through the locked door.

"I'm looking for Dr. Dillon Collins?" the unknown visitor
yelled.

"Who are you?" she asked as she wiped the sleep from her eyes
so she could see through the peephole.

"Are you Mrs. Collins?" the stranger asked.

"Yes."

"Mrs. Collins, I'm Officer Riddle with the Charleston Police
Department, and I need to talk to Dr. Collins."

Darcy struggled to unlock the door as she recognized the
badge the officer was holding to the peephole. Once the officer was
inside, Darcy showed him to the sofa. "Why do you need to see my
husband?"

"Ma'am, I'm investigating an incident and need to talk with
him as soon as possible."

"What kind of incident?" she asked, ignoring his request.

"Mrs. Collins, I'm not trying to be rude, but I really must see
him."

"He wasn't in bed, but let me check his office. Sometimes he
works late there," she said as she opened the office door. Seeing the
office was empty, she felt a skip in her heart. *Dillon, where are you?
Oh Lord, please let him be all right.* She turned to face the officer.
"He's not here. He left after dinner last night to help a friend. Is there
something I can do for you?" she asked, trying to keep her voice from
quivering.

"Mrs. Collins, we received a call last night regarding a domestic disturbance. Upon arriving on the scene, we noticed it appeared
there was a scuffle and some blood in the living room and outside the
home. No one was there, only a car. The tag came back registered to
Dr. Collins. I was wondering if he could tell us anything about the
situation," he explained.

Darcy stared in stunned silence at the officer sitting in front of her in the exact spot her sweet husband sat hours ago.

"Mrs. Collins, do you know where he is? Have you heard from him since he left?"

"No, no, I haven't," she said as she stood, crossed her arms, and began pacing the room. "He received a phone call from Cindy. Blood, whose blood?" she asked as she turned to face the officer.

"Who's Cindy?" he asked while recording the name on his notepad.

"She's a girl who recently moved here with her looser husband. She called and said something about her husband drinking again and hitting her again. Dillon said he had to go. Whose blood did you find? Is my husband okay?" she asked again, her voice louder than she intended.

"What's Cindy's husband's name? What do you know about them?" he asked as he continued making notes on his pad.

"They're just some couple who recently moved here from the Upstate, I believe. Um, either Greenville or Anderson. I think his name is Michael. Where is my husband!"

"Mrs. Collins, I don't know. We're just beginning our investigation. I'll let you know something as soon as I can. Now, what happened last night?" he asked as he motioned for her to sit on the sofa beside him.

"We got into an argument because he was leaving on our anniversary. I didn't even tell him goodbye," she said as a lump in her throat threatened to cut off her breath. *I didn't even tell him goodbye.*

"Mrs. Collins, who are Cindy and Michael?" he asked again.

"Cindy's a girl Dillon's been trying to help for the last two months. She and Michael moved into the little white house on Ashley Avenue. I don't know much about him except he's an alcoholic and physically abusive when he is drinking. Yet she's afraid to leave him. What type of woman stays with a man who's abusive?"

Ignoring her last question, he asked, "Do you know their last name?"

"I don't recall their last name, but they haven't been here long," she mechanically explained as she tried to figure out where her husband could be. "Have you checked with Dillon's office at the hospital? He may have gone there to check on the little girl involved in an accident earlier." *Why would he want to come home to an angry wife?*

"No, I haven't. This is the first place I've checked."

"I'll try to call him," she said as she shook her head trying to clear her thoughts. She reached for the phone and automatically dialed the number. After numerous rings, a lady finally answered, "Hey, this is Darcy, Dr. Collins's wife. Is he in the office?" After receiving the disappointing news, she hung up and turned to the officer, her face a ghostly white. The room began to spin, the officer moving farther and farther away as everything started to fade. Darcy collapsed. The officer caught her and placed her limp body on the cream leather couch in the living room.

Darcy awakened, hoping it was all a terrible dream. Peering into the unfamiliar green eyes of Officer Riddle, she realized it was really happening.

"Mrs. Collins, are you okay?" he asked. "I'll call for an ambulance. You may want to go to the hospital and have everything checked out. You don't look well."

Not hearing anything the officer said, Darcy asked, "You said there was blood, whose blood? Where was it? How much was there? What happened?"

"Ma'am, I don't know. We're still investigating the situation. That's why we need to talk with Dr. Collins. When he comes home, please have him call me immediately. Here's my card," he said as he handed her the small business card he removed from his wallet.

Stunned, Darcy sat on the sofa, staring at the table where Dillon set the medical bag when he came home yesterday.

The officer rose and left. After he closed the door behind him, a piece of paper on the table floated to the floor.

Darcy watched the paper as it made its decent. She rose from the sofa and walked toward it. Looking down at the paper, she noticed Dillon's writing. She bent and picked up the little note. *Darling, I'm sorry our anniversary turned out this way. I love you more than life itself. Please understand saving people is my job, and sometimes, my job can't wait. I love you and hope we can start over when I return home. I'll love you forever. Dillon.* Darcy held the note close to her heart and returned to the sofa, tears streaming down her face as she screamed, "Dillon, where are you? I'm so sorry, please come home to me. Lord, where's my husband?"

*****

The morning sun warmed Steve's unshaven face as he wandered the streets, following the scent of fresh-baked muffins—a scent he hadn't smelled since waking in his grandmother's house. Spotting the source of the alluring aroma, he smiled and walked into the quaint little restaurant called The Baker's Cafe.

Sitting before him in a glass case were an array of muffins, every flavor he could imagine. As he closed his eyes, he could see the tiny bedroom he shared with his sister, waking to the smell of fresh-baked muffins drifting from his grandmother's kitchen, her sweet voice singing "Amazing Grace" as she prepared for the day.

Steve was jolted from his reverie when the bell jingled and another customer entered the café. He placed his order and waited at the end of the counter until it was ready.

After picking up his food, Steve walked to a secluded table beside a window with a view of the shops on King Street. He was enjoying his morning as he watched people pass, some in a hurry and some just meandering along, enjoying the warm, windy day. Lynyrd Skynyrd's "Freebird" played over the speakers in the bakery. *Granny, I hope you still love this bird even though I don't think I could ever live for that Jesus fellow you keep talking about. Besides, who wants to be tied down to church and all those rules. I need to be me...I need to be free.*

*****

Darcy's fingers traced the wrinkles of the worn leather Bible beside the sofa—the same Bible Dillon studied every morning. *Lord, I can't get through this alone. Please give me strength and wisdom. Dillon's always talking about Your grace. I need Your grace now. I need*

*You. I want my husband back!* she prayed as she opened the Bible to the place Dillon had marked the morning before.

"And we know all things work together for good to those who love God, to those who are called according to His purpose," Darcy read the verse over and over, seeking to understand how this situation could ever work for good. *Lord, I don't know what your plan is, but I know Dillon trusts You, and he always said You are always in control. I trust You'll help me find Dillon.* After her prayer, she rose from the sofa, washed her face, and went for a walk, hoping to understand how a loving God would allow such a horrible situation.

*\*\*\*\*\**

As he continued to eat, Steve watched the people pass until a tired and disoriented-looking young lady caught his attention. He watched as she walked through the doors of the café.

The dark-haired woman stood in the doorway. Moments later, she ran her fingers through her muddled hair and proceeded to the counter. Steve watched as she made her way to a table in the back corner. She sat in a wooden chair and seemed to be frozen in time. Her face showed trails of tears, her eyes red and baggy from a lack of sleep, or was it worry? A lump rose in Steve's throat as his heart ached for the downhearted woman. *What happened to her?* he wondered as he continued to observe the troubled lady.

Steve sat gazing at her, his heart urging him to approach her, but his pride stopping him. *At least see if she needs something. No, what if she thinks I'm crazy? You could be her last hope. She might think I'm just some jerk coming on to her.* The battle inside his head continued. He stood and walked toward her. His palms sweating, he stopped by the trash bin and placed his garbage inside. She never stirred. He felt as if his heart were beating in his throat. He could hardly breathe. Overcome with anxiety, Steve rushed from the café.

*\*\*\*\*\**

21

After a long day of shopping, Steve was thrilled to see the door to his hotel room, at least until he realized he left his key locked inside. He looked up and down the hall for housekeeping, but no one was around. After stacking his gifts by the door, Steve walked toward the elevators. Once there, he reached for the house phone and called the service desk. A few moments later, he returned to his packages and waited for the manager to come up with an extra key. Ten minutes later, he was finally in his room. He placed the packages on the dresser and collapsed onto the bed, contemplating his next move. It didn't take long before his stomach began reminding him the only food he had eaten today was the muffin from this morning, and it was long gone. He rose; showered and shaved his scruffy face, then dressed for dinner. He placed his hand on the knob, anticipating a pleasant meal but couldn't open the door. He stood frozen as he remembered his promise to call his grandmother when he returned. With a heavy sigh, he turned and stared at the beckoning phone. He walked to it and dialed the familiar number, hoping he would be greeted with her answering machine. After several rings, he heard the sweet, fragile voice of his loving grandmother.

"Hello?" the frail voice echoed in his head. "Hello?" she repeated.

Unable to utter a word, he hung up. He sat on the bed for what seemed like an eternity, stunned at how fragile her voice sounded. Convincing himself he would call her after dinner, he rose and quickly left the room.

# CHAPTER 3

*Kansas City, Kansas*

Dillon felt like a trapped animal. His eyes searched for a way to escape as he wiggled his hands side-to-side, trying to break free from the ropes that bound him. His shoulders ached from the constant motion. The car stopped. Dillon lay still, listening for any indication of where he was, but all he could hear was the song they kept playing over and over, the words continuously running through his thoughts. *If I hear that song one more time, I'm going to scream. Lord, help me. Get me out of here. I can't take this much longer. Lord, I know You're with me and will never leave me or forsake me. Please protect me and give me wisdom during this ordeal...*

"And if you love him, oh be proud of him, cause after all he's just a man. Stand by your man..."

*Oh, please help me get this crazy song out of my head,* he screamed as he continued to pray. *Bless Darcy, Lord, I know she'll be worried and looking for me. Give her strength and peace.* His prayer was interrupted when Michael opened the trunk.

"What's wrong, doctor man, you can't save yourself?" he asked, chuckling as he stared at the battered doctor, legs and arms tied and mouth gagged. "This is what happens when you stick your nose in another man's business." He sneered and then looked over the top of the trunk. "Cindy, get over here and help get this worthless doctor out of the trunk," he yelled. "And turn that stupid song off. I'm tired of hearing it."

Dillon heard the passenger door open, and the music abruptly cut off. Cindy appeared at her husband's side. They pulled Dillon from the trunk. His legs ached from being cramped for hours in the small trunk of the blue Monarch. They released him, and he fell onto the cold concrete floor of the garage.

"Grab that chair over yonder and help me put him in it," Michael said as he shoved Cindy in the direction of the chair. She stumbled but regained her step and brought the chair closer to Dillon. The two of them dragged Dillon to the rickety metal chair, dropping his battered body onto the seat. Michael quickly secured his legs to the legs of the chair. Then without wasting any time, he grabbed the other chair. The noise of the metal scrapping the concrete caused Cindy to jump.

"Sit down," he commanded as he placed the other chair to the back of Dillon's. She did as she was ordered.

"Michael, what're you doing?" Cindy asked.

Dillon winced at the sharp smack accompanied by Cindy's scream. She began sobbing quietly. With a glance over his shoulder, Dillon saw Michael lashing Cindy's legs to her chair in the same manner that his own had been tied. The drunk glanced up and caught him watching and spit at him.

"Michael, please," Cindy whispered. Michael's rough footsteps and the slamming of the garage door were the only reply.

A few hours later, Michael returned with a paper bag. He sat the bag on the trunk of the car and then untied his wife, grabbed her already bruised arm, and shoved her in the direction of the bag.

Dillon could tell by his stumbling walk that Michael had had more to drink. From his chair, he watched as Michael removed two sandwiches and two bottles of water from the bag, Cindy standing next to him, hugging her arms. Her eyes darted from the food to her husband. She stood as a statue while her husband devoured his food, and Dillon's heart ached as he realized why she was hesitating. She was waiting for permission.

Michael looked at her and then at the untouched food. "Eat!" he said as crumbs of bread fell from his overly full mouth onto his gruffy, oily beard.

She jumped at his voice. Grabbing the sandwich, she crammed the food into her mouth. Then Michael turned to Dillon. The doctor tried to straighten up in his chair as the man staggered over. Michael ripped the tape from Dillon's mouth, and Dillon yelped.

His lips stung as he clasped them together, biting back another wince. "You're not going to get away with this," Dillon said.

"That's what you think, doctor man. I've already gotten away with it," Michael said with a smile on his face, revealing rotting teeth and acrid breath. "Bring a sandwich and water over here," he yelled, looking at his wife.

Cindy rushed to grab the food and water and do as she was told. She stood beside Michael, waiting for her husband's next order.

"Are you really that stupid? Do I have to tell you everything?" he said as he shoved her toward Dillon. "Feed the doctor man so we can get some sleep."

She unwrapped the sandwich and started breaking it into small pieces. Dillon could feel his lips swelling. "I'm so sorry," Cindy said as she placed the first morsel in his mouth.

He tried to chew. Pain shot through his jaw as he tried to eat the food she offered. He couldn't decide which was worse, his hunger or the pain it caused to eat, but he knew he had to keep his strength up if he was going to make it out of this situation.

"Dr. Collins, I'm sorry I got you into this," she said as she offered him some water.

"Cindy, it's not your fault. You didn't know he was coming home early. If we had left a few minutes earlier, you would've been at the shelter. Can't you see this situation is his fault?" Dillon said.

"No, Dr. Collins. If I hadn't made him mad to begin with, he never would've hit me. I just never know when to shut up." She offered him more food as she looked at the floor, avoiding Dillon's eyes.

"No talking!" Michael yelled from the garage door. "Hurry up and feed him. I have things to do."

She obeyed, and when she completed the task, she picked up the trash from the food wrappers.

"Sit down," he barked and pointed to the chair behind Dillon once again.

"Michael, it's not necessary to tie me up. I'm not going anywhere. I love you," she begged as she walked toward the chair anyway with her head hung down, exhaling heavily. The chair clattered when Michael shoved her into the seat and tied her to the cold metal that would be her bed for the night. "Michael, please don't do this. I love you, and I'm not going anywhere. I'd never leave you."

Dillon heard the rip of duct tape, and Cindy's voice was silenced. A moment later, Michael's glaring eyes were before him, and another piece of tape covered Dillon's burning lips.

*****

## Charleston, South Carolina

Darcy stood on the steps of her home after spending the day walking numbly down the streets of Charleston. The brick steps led to the large wraparound porch adorned with black iron rails, making it one of the prettiest homes in Charleston. As beautiful as the house was, it did not soothe the loneliness and pain she felt as she quietly walked through the door.

It was late and she was exhausted, but she couldn't make herself walk into their room. The room they talked in; the room they laughed in; the room they loved in—their room. She grabbed the blanket off the back of the couch, lay down, and curled herself into a tight little ball, sobbing for her missing love. Sleep took its time but finally came, and she drifted into a world of darkness.

*****

Replaying that night over and over in his mind only made him anxious. Resolute in his promise to call her, Steve sat on the edge of the bed. Shame filled his heart as he remembered the harsh words he said to his dear, sweet granny. Lifting the receiver, he dialed her number once again.

"Hello?" the loving, frail voice of his grandmother answered after the third ring.

His heart pounding in his chest, his palms sweating, he inhaled and said, "Hi, Granny, it's me, Steve." It seemed an eternity before Steve heard a response from his grandmother.

"Stevie?" she asked. "Is it really you?"

"Yes, Granny, it's me. Please don't hang up," he said quickly, afraid she would reject him before he could try to make things right with the woman who raised him. "I have so much to tell you. I want to apologize—"

Interrupting his planned speech, she said without hesitation, "Stevie, I've missed you so much. I've been praying for you since the day you left. How are you?" Tears flowed from his eyes.

*I should have known she'd love me no matter what.* "I'm okay. I'm in Charleston and would love to see you."

"How soon can you come home?" she asked as if nothing ever happened.

*Home, she still considered her place his home.* "I'd love to come home if you'll have me."

"Sweetheart, I've prayed for this day since the day you left. Come home as soon as you can!" she answered, gasping between sobs.

"How's tomorrow?" he asked, overwhelmed by her love.

"I can't wait. I'll cook your favorite meal, and we can catch up then. I love you, Stevie. I knew Jesus would answer my prayers and bring you home."

"I know, Granny. I love you too." *Your Jesus had nothing to do with it. I just hate the way I treated you and want to make it right,* he thought as he paused before he began his apology. "I'm sorry. I can't wait to see you." Pain filled his voice as tears fell from his eyes; his throat tightened, threatening to cut off his air. "I'll see you tomorrow," Steve said as he hung up the phone and sat on the bed, weeping over lost years and his treatment of his loving, forgiving grandmother.

*****

## Kansas City, Kansas

Dillon and Cindy roused at the squeak of the driver's door as Michael emerged from the car.

"Sleep well?" Michael asked with a sneer on his face. Neither captive moved as he meandered toward them, the stench from his unwashed body reaching them first. "When I untie you, open the trunk and place the rope by the chair. Then get in the passenger's seat and keep your mouth shut," he ordered as he yanked the tape from Cindy's mouth.

"Ouch," she cried, tears filling her eyes. She rose and complied with his orders. She placed the rope beside the chair and went to the passenger seat, never opening her mouth. The car bounced, and Cindy knew the injured doctor had been forced into the trunk—the small dark box that would be his home until they stopped once again.

# CHAPTER 4

*Charleston, South Carolina*

Steve rose early the next morning, anxiety surging through him. After gathering the towel for his shower, he entered the bathroom and tossed it toward the toilet seat. He gripped the knob and turned the water on as thoughts of his grandmother ran through his head. The hot water cascaded over his body as he sang "Amazing Grace," the words meaning nothing to him, just a song he remembered his grandmother singing while cooking their breakfast. When he stepped out of the shower, the cold air covered his body like a blanket. His eyes widened as he reached for his towel. "Crap!" he yelled, looking at the white porcelain toilet bowl and the towel that sat inside, completely soaked. Water pooled around his feet as he searched for a fresh towel. After he was finally able to dress and clean up his mess in the bathroom, he turned on the television to listen to the news while he packed for the trip home.

Steve rushed from his room, ready to begin his trip to Greenville. The sky was an angry gray; it felt like it could rain at any moment. He was so glad his friend had been able to bring his car to Charleston after he disembarked at the battery. He hurried to load the car, hoping to leave before the storm arrived.

*****

29

The hour was early. Darkness covered the sky. The ringing of the phone jarred Darcy from her fitful sleep on the sofa. "Hello?" she said, her voice raspy from sleep.

"Darcy, it's Cindy," she said in a barely audible whisper.

"Where are you? How's Dillon? Can I talk to him?" Darcy asked, struggling to keep her composure.

"We're okay. Dillon and I are both hurt, but we're okay. I can't talk long. Michael's gone for food, and I found a phone in the garage," she explained. "We're traveling west. The last sign I read said we're entering Kansas City." Cindy paused. "I have to go, he's coming," she quickly said as she hung up the phone.

"No!" Darcy screamed only to be answered by silence. "No!" she yelled again, slamming the phone onto the receiver. "Lord, help me! Where is he? Why are You doing this to me?" she cried out. She sobbed and punched the arm of the sofa over and over until she was exhausted. Suddenly, she picked up the phone and dialed the number from the card sitting on the table.

"How may I direct your call?" the nasally voice on the other end asked.

"Officer Riddle, please. Tell him it's Darcy Collins."

"I'm sorry, Mrs. Collins, but Officer Riddle isn't here at the moment. Would you like his voicemail?"

"No, I need to speak to someone immediately concerning the disappearance of my husband," Darcy snapped.

"Hold on, please," was the only reply she received before being transferred to another person.

After holding for what felt like an eternity, Darcy was forwarded to the Missing Persons Department. "Missing Persons, may I help you?"

"This is Darcy Collins, and I just received a call from Cindy Hogan. I'd like to speak with Officer Riddle about my husband who's missing," she explained, trying hard to keep from screaming at the seemingly uncaring person on the other end.

"Oh, Mrs. Collins, hold on, and I'll transfer you to his cell phone. He's been hoping you'd call."

After three rings, the deep voice she'd been trying to reach was finally on the other end of the phone. "Officer Riddle."

"Hey, it's Darcy. Cindy just called," she said, panic filling her voice.

"Did she say where they are?"

"Kansas City is the last sign she saw. She told me that she and Dillon were hurt but okay. She also told me Michael was gone for food. When he left, she found a phone in the garage and used it to call me. What are you going to do?"

"For now, I'll give the information to the detectives working the case and see if they can find any relatives he may be running to."

"Thanks, Officer Riddle. I'll call you if I hear from them," she said as she returned the receiver to the cradle. She sank into the sofa, curled into a ball, and stared at the phone, lost in thoughts of her precious Dillon.

# CHAPTER 5

*Greenville, South Carolina*

As Steve pulled onto the two-lane, tree-lined street, he was taken back to his carefree childhood. A time when all he worried about was his next adventure and not being late for dinner. He parked in front of the small olive-green house surrounded by the smoky gray chain-link fence. He sat in his neglected blue '75 Gran Torino, trying to calm his shaking hands.

His grandmother waited, pacing the screened-in porch until the young man emerged from the car. "Stevie!" she yelled as she shuffled from the porch to meet him.

His huge muscular arms wrapped around the tiny elderly woman he had so dearly missed. They stood in the middle of the small yard, clinging to each other as tears flowed from both faces, neither able to speak.

Steve took a deep breath, breaking the everlasting hug, and put his arm around his grandmother's shoulders. "Granny, it's been a long time, and there's so much I need to tell you. Can we talk over lunch?"

"Oh, yes! I made your favorite meal, pot roast with those little white potatoes you like," she exclaimed as she led him through the living room and dining room into the warm pale-yellow kitchen where he had enjoyed many meals with this precious woman.

Once seated, Steve piled his plate with food, ready to devour the meal. He raised his head, and his eyes met his granny's. A soft smile pulled at her lips as she reached for his hand. *How could I forget? She always prays before we eat.* He held her hand and bowed his head as she prayed to her God. As soon as the prayer was over, Steve dug in. Moments later, he realized he hadn't spoken to his grandmother since beginning their meal.

"The food is great, Granny. It's been a long time since I've had such a delicious home-cooked dinner," he said with a smile.

"Well, how was the Navy?"

"It was okay. I really enjoyed the time I spent at the Naval Regional Medical Center."

His grandmother looked at him when he mentioned the medical center. "I didn't know you were into the medical field. I thought you were an officer."

"I am an officer," he explained. "I just really admired the doctors and the work they were doing at the medical center. Before I left Charleston, I called my commander and asked about transferring to the medical field myself."

"Oh Stevie!" she exclaimed. "You would make a wonderful doctor."

A blush dusted his cheeks as she continued to rave about how great he would be.

"I wish I had the confidence in me that you do."

She laid her hand upon his shoulder as an affectionate smile covered her face. "Honey, I know you can do anything you desire as long as you trust in God."

A cloud rumbled behind Steve's eyes at the mention of God. *How can I trust someone who took my parents away when I was a child? I needed them.* Determined not to allow his feelings about God cause this visit to turn into another argument, he decided to change the subject. "How's Cindy? I haven't seen or talked to her since I left for the Navy."

"I suppose she's fine. She met this man named Michael Hogan in March, and they married in June. I haven't heard from her since the wedding."

"Wedding?" Steve asked. "That was quick."

She nodded her head in agreement. "Yeah, and I'm not sure about him. She was angry with me when they moved to Charleston after the ceremony. He seemed cold to me, but you know your sister, she's stubborn and has always done what she wants regardless of what you try to tell her." She paused and laughed as she said, "Sort of like her brother."

Steve laughed with his grandmother. She rose from her chair and began clearing the table. He rose to help her. "No, no. I'll take care of washing everything later," she said as she swatted his hands. "I'm just going to clear the dishes right now. I have a special dessert for you."

"You didn't?" Steve asked as a smile covered his face.

"You take the coffee into the living room and turn on the television. I'll bring dessert."

He turned and picked up the coffee pot and cups and walked to the living room. *I can't believe she's forgiven me so easily. She acts like it never happened, even making my favorite dessert on top of it all.* His thoughts were interrupted by the smell of the tasty treat. "Granny, I can't believe you baked that just for me," he said as he stood to help her. The sparkle in her eyes and smile on her face caused his heart to ache even more knowing how he treated her the night he left.

"Honey, I couldn't let you come home and not have rice pudding ready," she said as she sat beside him on the couch. Both settled next to each other, enjoying their dessert as the news came on.

"This is a breaking news alert. Charleston police are looking for these three people: Michael and Cindy Hogan and Dr. Dillon Collins. We currently have few details but know Michael Hogan is a suspect in the disappearance of Dr. Collins. It's unknown at this time if Cindy Hogan is a victim or if she is connected to the disappearance also. If you've seen these people, contact the Charleston Police Department immediately. Do not approach them. They may be armed and dangerous."

Steve stared at the pictures on the television, the spoonful of pudding frozen in midair.

"Steve, that's Cindy," Granny said as she laid her hand on Steve's arm.

Steve returned the spoon to the dish. He turned to face his sobbing grandmother. "I'll find her, Granny. I promise."

"Do you think Cindy's involved?" she asked, her hands trembling along with her voice.

"No, Granny. Cindy couldn't hurt anyone," he said as he took the little old lady in his arms and hugged her close. "I'm going to go back to Charleston and see if I can find out what's going on."

"I'll be praying for you, honey. Please call me when you find her."

Steve rose from the couch, left his dishes on the table, and walked toward the front door, followed by his grandmother. When Steve reached the door, he turned and kissed his grandmother on top of her hair. "I'll call as soon as I can."

"I'll be praying."

"You do that. It looks like she'll need all the help she can get right now," he said as he turned and ran toward his car.

*****

## Oakley, Idaho

Most everything was quiet in Oakley as the car pulled into the garage at nearly two in the morning.

"What's going on?" the question was barked out in anger.

Dillon lay quiet in the dark trunk, intently listening for any clues as to where he could be. *Who is that?* he thought when he heard the strange deep voice.

"Shut up and give me time to get out of the car," Michael yelled back as the driver door opened with the familiar squeak. "Stay in the car," he bellowed, the car shaking as he got out. "Hey bro, come back here and help me."

Dillon could hear two sets of footsteps making their way to where he lay. The click of the lock sent shivers down his spine. *What torment awaits me now?* he thought as the trunk was raised. Dillon slowly opened his eyes, trying to adjust to the light in the garage, a useless action this time. The room was dark. The only light he could see was in the far corner. *Where am I?* he thought as Michael and a scruffy large man jerked him from the trunk.

"What have you done?" the scruffy man asked.

"It doesn't matter. Now I have to decide what to do with him," Michael stated as the two men let go of Dillon, who immediately fell.

Dillon lay on the cold concrete, staring at the two men.

"Where can I put him until I decide what to do?" Michael asked.

"You can't keep him here!" the scruffy man yelled. "I don't want to be part of this."

"I just need a day or two, then we'll be out of here."

"Okay," he said as he looked around the room. Moments passed like hours. He cleared his throat and continued, "You can put him in the cellar but only for a day or two."

The two men grabbed Dillon by the arms and hauled him to the cold, damp cellar, his legs bouncing off each step.

"There, over in the corner's fine. I can tie him to the rails," Michael said, nodding his head in the direction he wished to go. Dillon was carried to the corner and secured with rope. Both men left without a word, locking the door behind them. Dillon sat alone, cold, and hungry. *Lord, why have you left me? What am I supposed to do?* he prayed, tuning out the sound of mice scurrying nearby.

# CHAPTER 6

*Charleston, South Carolina*

When Steve awoke, it was late morning, and the maids bustled around the halls at The Fultan Lane Inn, cleaning the rooms. He rubbed his eyes and pushed his tired body from the bed. He sat there until he felt awake enough to shower and shave. *What am I going to do? Where do I start?*

*****

Rising from the sofa, she stumbled to the bathroom, retching all the way.

*Lord, what am I going to do? I can't go on. I feel so hopeless. It's more than I can bear. I'm worrying myself sick. Please, ease my hurt and bring my Dillon home.* It took her a moment to realize the phone was ringing. Shaking her head as if clearing the memories from last night's call, she picked up the receiver. "Hello?"

"Hey, Darcy, how are you this morning?" Pastor Watson asked, his voice full of kindness and concern.

"I'm okay. I feel so tired and nauseous. I was just praying when you called."

"Darcy, I'm so sorry you are going through so much. I hope you know we are all praying for you. If you need anything, please let me know."

*Praying for me? You should be praying for Dillon.* "I appreciate the prayers, Pastor Watson."

"Dillon is a man of Christ, and I know God will be with him." Silence filled the air as he waited for a response which never came. After clearing his throat, he proceeded. "I know you're going through a great deal, and I hesitate to ask for your assistance, but we had an emergency situation arise last night," he continued.

"What happened?"

"I received a call from the Department of Social Services yesterday. They have a six-year-old little girl whose father was killed in an auto accident a few days ago. As of today, they haven't been able to find any of her family."

"Oh, I wonder if it's the same little girl Dillon told me about?" she asked as a lump formed in the back of her throat. Memories of her conversation played through her mind as she rubbed her burning eyes, tired from the sleepless night.

"It's possible. Her name is Hope. There's no place for Hope in the foster system at the moment. She stayed with me last night. Since I'm a single man, I feel very inadequate taking care of a small child," he continued, not giving Darcy a chance to question him further. "Mary from DSS said she would look at her list of foster parents and place her with one of them as soon as a spot becomes available. I remembered you and Dillon had mentioned wanting to be foster parents. I prayed about this situation for hours last night and told Mary about you this morning. She suggested I call you. If you're willing to take the little girl, I'm supposed to call her back so she can make a home visit. Would you be willing to take care of her? At least for a little while until DSS can find another alternative?"

"I was wondering what happened to her. I'm just not sure I'm up to taking care of her right now with all that's going on. I really need to focus on finding Dillon."

"I understand, Darcy. Would you be able to help for just a few days? Maybe a relative will be found soon."

"Pastor Watson, can I think about it over coffee and call you in an hour or so? I just woke up, and I don't feel I'm in any condition to make a good decision right now," she added, trying to absorb the sad story he just told her.

"Sure, that'll be great. I'll pray for you, Darcy, and look forward to your call soon. By the way, have you heard anything yet concerning Dillon?"

"Cindy called yesterday and said they were okay, and she thought they were in Kansas. She hung up before I could find out anything further," she said as she took a deep breath, trying to calm her nausea.

"Please, let me know if there's anything I can do. I'll be praying for you both."

"Thank you," Darcy said and replaced the receiver on the cradle, then walked toward the kitchen. When she reached the counter, she grabbed the glass pot and poured a cup of coffee and sat at the kitchen table to pray. *Lord, what do you want me to do? I'm hurting so much right now. I can't even take care of myself, let alone a child. What am I supposed to do? What kind of world is this, Lord? My husband's missing, and You take away this little girl's father. The Bible says You are a God of love. What kind of love is that? With that kind of love, what kind of hope is there for this horrible world?* Continuing to sip her coffee, she began to wonder, *What would Dillon do if he were here?* Knowing Dillon's loving, giving heart, she knew what she must do. She picked up the phone and dialed the pastor's number.

"Hello?"

"Hey, Pastor Watson, it's Darcy."

"Hey, Darcy. I didn't expect to hear from you so quickly."

"I've been thinking about our conversation, and yes, I'd love to take care of Hope for a little while."

"Oh, Darcy, that's wonderful. You're such a blessing. This precious little girl needs the love and understanding of someone who knows how she feels, and I feel you'll do a wonderful job with her." Joy filled his voice as they made plans to bring Hope to her new and loving temporary home. Pastor Watson ended the conversation hoping the girls would help each other heal their shattered lives.

# CHAPTER 7

*Charleston, South Carolina*

The hot water caressed his back as Steve stood in the shower, contemplating how to find his sister. Thoughts of where she could be running through his mind as he turned the shower off and stepped out onto the cold tile of the bathroom floor. Steve felt energized after a hot shower. He put on his naval uniform hoping people would be more willing to talk with a sailor than a stranger. After checking his appearance in the mirror one last time, he left the room, heading to the quaint café which made those wonderful muffins. He knew it would be a long day searching for his sister, and he needed all the strength he could muster.

*****

"Good morning, Darcy. This is Hope," Pastor Watson introduced the ladies as Darcy opened the front door. She smiled at the adorable girl with wavy coal-black hair falling past her shoulders, reminding her of Dillon.

"Hey, my name's Darcy," she greeted the little girl with sea-green eyes that matched her own. *Hope, what a beautiful name.* Darcy prayed as she led her visitors to the den. *Lord, I guess You do send hope when we're in despair. How awesome You are. Please help me be who I need to be for this little one You sent to me.*

"Hope," Pastor Watson addressed the small figure sitting on the sofa. "Darcy's going to take care of you for a while. She loves children and can understand how you feel."

Hope sat with her fist clenched tightly in her lap, her face red from the tears. Sensing Hope's loneliness, Darcy sat next to her, placing her arm around the little girl's slumped shoulders and her other hand under her chin, lifting her small head until their eyes met. "Hope, sweetheart, I know you're hurting. I can't imagine how you must feel. If there's anything I can do for you or anything I can get you, please let me know."

"No one can get me what I want. I want my daddy," she said as she threw herself into Darcy's arms, weeping uncontrollably. Darcy's heart melted as she held the grief-stricken little girl.

Pastor Watson stood and watched as Darcy held Hope and gently rocked her as the girl's sobs subsided. "I've got an idea, why don't we walk to The Baker's Café and I'll buy muffins and juice for everyone."

The girls smiled. "That would be fun," Darcy said. She and Hope stood up simultaneously and headed for the door.

*****

## Oakley, Idaho

"What have I done?" he screamed when he saw the black-and-blue bruising on his wife's face as she handed him his morning coffee.

"Michael, you've been drunk for five days. Honey, don't you remember what happened?"

"No, I don't. Are you okay?" he asked, alarm filled his voice.

"I will be, but I'm not sure about Dr. Collins."

"Doctor who?" he asked, his brows knitted and eyes squinted.

"Oh my!" she gasped. "You really don't remember, do you?"

He placed his head in his hands and slowly shook it back and forth.

"Michael, you came home drunk Friday. We started arguing, and you hit me again. After you left, I called Dr. Collins to help me. When you came back home, he was there, and you hit him in the back of the head and the ribs with the fire poker. He collapsed, and you tied him up," she explained, trying to fill in all the missing pieces of Michael's memory. "Then you drank four more beers and began to panic as you watched Dr. Collins start to come to. Before he could wake up, you hit him in the head again and drug him to the car and placed him in the trunk. After that, you shoved me into the car, and we took off."

"Where's he now? Is he alive?"

"He was still alive when we left him Monday morning in the cellar."

"What day is it?"

"Tuesday afternoon."

All the color drained from Michael's face as the reality of what he had done struck him. Tears began to flow from his eyes, and the shame he felt showed on his unshaven face. He grabbed his wife and held her. "Cindy, I'm so sorry," he pleaded. "Please forgive me."

"Honey, I always do," she said as she relished the feeling of being comforted by his arms. "We must get medical help for Dr. Collins and find a way to get him home." she said, taking advantage of his soft, sober side.

"You're right but how?"

"I don't know, but let's talk it over with your brother," she said as his brother entered the room.

*****

## Charleston, South Carolina

His first day back to Charleston was spectacular but lost on Steve. The August sun was hot over a cloudless sky, and the wind gently blew, caressing each person it touched. He entered the café and ordered a muffin and coffee. The restaurant was crowded, and only two tables were unoccupied. Steve sat at the table closest to the door and began reading the daily paper.

The café door opened, and the laughter of a young girl filled the room. Steve looked over the top of his paper and watched as the girl animatedly talked with the two grown-ups with her. He quickly recognized the woman as the sad dark-haired woman who entered the café on Saturday. *That must be her husband and daughter,* he thought as he continued to read the paper.

The trio placed their order and settled at the table beside Steve.

A shrill ring emanated from the woman's purse. "Hello," she said as she pulled the phone from her purse and answered it. "Hey Officer Riddle. No, I haven't heard anything from Dillon or Cindy since she called Monday."

The mention of Cindy's name piqued Steve's attention. He kept the paper at reading level, hoping not to get caught listening but desperate to know whether she could be talking about his sister.

"Yes, sir, I can meet you at the police department. How about in ten minutes? Great. I'll see you then," she said as she placed her phone in her purse.

"Pastor Watson, can you watch Hope for a little while? I need to meet Officer Riddle at the police department. He said he has some information concerning Dillon's disappearance."

"Of course. Just call me when you're finished, and I'll bring Hope home."

Darcy rose and hugged them both as she left the café.

Steve got up, tossed his garbage into the trash bin, and followed Darcy. "Excuse me, lady!" he yelled as he rushed beside her. "I'm sorry, but I couldn't help but overhear your conversation. I heard you mention the name Cindy."

Darcy stopped in her tracks. Her piercing emerald eyes fixed on the face of the unknown man. "What about her?"

Steve stuck his hand out as he introduced himself. "My name is Steve Parnell, and Cindy's my sister's name. I came to Charleston to find her."

Darcy made no move to shake his hand; she turned to continue her journey to the police department. "If your sister is the same

Cindy I referred to, you really don't wish to speak to me because she and her husband have kidnapped my husband," she yelled as she quickened her pace. "Now, leave me alone."

Undeterred by the upset woman, Steve followed her to the police station, hoping to find his baby sister.

*****

## Oakley, Idaho

"You got the medical bag?"

"I have it," the voice answered with apparent anxiety.

"Hurry up. I don't want him to die."

"Be patient, man. I can't walk any faster. I'm old, and these knees don't move as quick as they use to."

Michael opened the cellar door. The foursome was met with the stench of sewage and body odor. The old doctor had to suppress the desire to heave.

"He's over here." Michael motioned as he rushed toward the lifeless body.

*****

## Charleston, South Carolina

Darcy entered the police department with Steve on her heels. "Hi, I'm Darcy Collins, and I'm here to see Officer Riddle," she said to the receptionist behind the glass partition.

"We're here to see Officer Riddle," Steve corrected before either lady could reply.

Darcy turned and glared at him. "This is none of your business."

"It is my business if the Cindy you referred to is my sister, Cindy Hogan," he barked back with his hands on his hips, meeting her glare for glare.

Her face grew red with anger; she clenched her teeth and pursed her lips. The only sound he heard was the low growl she made as she turned to face Office Riddle who was coming through the door.

"Hey, Darcy," Officer Riddle said. Hesitation filled his voice as he neared the waiting couple.

Darcy turned her attention to the approaching officer. "Have you heard anything?"

Unsure of the stranger beside her, Officer Riddle ignored her question. "Who's this?" he asked, looking at Steve.

"I don't know. He said his name is Steve," she said as she turned and scowled at the man behind her. "He followed me from the café, saying he's Cindy's brother."

Nodding his head slowly as that piece of information registered in his thoughts, he opened the door for Darcy and Steve.

Before Darcy could move, Steve took a step forward and stuck his hand out toward the officer. "I'm Steve Parnell and my sister, Cindy Hogan, is missing. I couldn't get an answer from this woman so I followed her here to see what I could find out."

"Let's go into the conference room and I will fill you both in on what we know so far," he suggested.

# CHAPTER 8

*Oakley, Idaho*

Michael and his brother carried the limp body upstairs, placing him on the bed. He was filthy from the top of his head down to his black dress shoes. Blood stained the once nice white dress shirt and black designer slacks he wore.

The old doctor pushed past the two brothers to check on the patient. "His breathing is shallow. He needs to be cleaned up so I can look at all of the wounds, the wounds to his head especially."

Upon hearing the doctor's advice, Michael turned to Cindy, his eyes wide with fear. His hands shook, a constant reminder of how desperately he wanted, needed a drink. "Go to the kitchen and get some clean water and towels so we can clean him up. Check the house for any first aid supplies available and hurry!" he said as he stood, running his hands through his oily hair and pacing floor.

She swiftly left the room, gathering the needed materials. *Lord, please help Dillon. Please don't let him die.* "Here's the water and towels," she said as she hurried to her husband's side and handed the items to him.

Less than thirty minutes passed before the men finished cleaning the wounds. "He's clean and ready for you, Doctor," Michael said as he turned and handed Cindy the dirty water and towels.

The doctor sat beside Dillon as Cindy, Michael, and his brother left the room, closing the door behind them. They sat at the wooden kitchen table while an uncomfortable silence filled the room. They waited anxiously for the doctor to return with information concerning the corpselike body in the bedroom just beyond the closed door.

"You know this wouldn't have happened if you didn't drink," his brother said in a matter-of-fact tone.

Unable to respond, Michael just nodded his head.

"You need to call the authorities and tell them what happened," he said as he continued trying to guide his brother to do the right thing. "God will help you through this."

Michael raised his head, his brown eyes filled with anger. "God? I don't need anyone to help me through this. God doesn't even know who I am," he bellowed, causing Cindy to flinch.

Confident her husband wouldn't hurt her while sober, she placed her hand on his tattooed arm. "Michael, don't say such a horrible thing. God knows who you are. He loves you. He loves everyone."

"If God loves me, then why am I in this situation?" he sneered sarcastically.

"Honey, God didn't put you in this situation. You made the decisions which put us here."

"Yeah, then why is Dr. Collins in the situation he's in? He didn't choose to be here."

"No, he didn't, but the Bible says it rains on the just and unjust. So only God knows why Dr. Collins is part of this."

The doctor emerged from the bedroom, all conversation ceased, and every eye looked toward him. "I don't know if he'll make it or not. He really needs to be in a hospital. I've done everything I know to do."

"Thank you, Doc," Michael said as he handed the old man a wad of cash. "We'll think about it."

"If you don't get him to a hospital, he won't make it," he said as he gathered his bag, pocketed the money, and left.

*****

47

## *Charleston, South Carolina*

"Officer Riddle, have you found anything out about my husband?" Darcy asked as she sat in the chair opposite Steve.

"Well, we know the blood found in the home is from two different people. We assume one blood type is Cindy's since you reported your husband was responding to her call for help. We now have confirmed through his records at the hospital, the other blood type is Dillon's."

The words of the officer faded from her ears as all the possibilities of what could have happened to her husband played in her mind.

"Darcy, did you hear what I said?" Officer Riddle asked, interrupting her runaway thoughts.

"What? No, I'm sorry. I didn't hear you. I was thinking about Dillon and what could have happened to him," she said as tears threatened to spill from her tormented eyes.

"We traced Michael's family records, and he has family in Idaho, but we didn't locate anyone in Kansas. Do you know anything about Michael's relatives?" he asked as he turned to face Steve.

Steve sat motionless in the cold metal chair, his face absent of color. "You said you found her blood, was there a lot of blood? Do you think she is alive?" he asked.

Officer Riddle ran his hand through his hair. "We don't know yet. Do you know anything about Michael's relatives?" he asked again.

"No," he said, shaking his head as he looked down at his hands, which were folded in his lap. "I don't even know him. All I know is my grandmother said my sister, Cindy, married Michael Hogan a couple of months ago and moved to Charleston. She hasn't heard from her since." Silence filled the room as Darcy and Officer Riddle looked at Steve. "What?" he asked when he noticed their stare.

"Well, you seem like you're a million miles away, and your jaw is open. I guess we're waiting to see what you were thinking," Office Riddle explained.

Steve closed his eyes, took a deep breath, and exhaled slowly. "I was just thinking about my family out west, but I don't think Cindy would go there."

"Where out west?"

"Where does your family live out west?" Darcy asked immediately on the heels of Officer Riddle's question, her voice higher than normal.

"I have an uncle who owns a feed lot in Idaho. Cindy's never met him, so I'd really be surprised if they were going there."

"We have to investigate any possibility. If you don't mind, please write down his information so we can contact him and at least make him aware of the situation. Until I hear from the investigators, that's all I have at this point."

"Thank you, Officer," Steve said as he stood, handing him the paper with his uncle Harley's information and shook his hand. Darcy followed his lead. They left the police department in complete silence. Tears trailed down Darcy's face as she struggled not to give in to the urge to collapse into a ball and disappear, hoping deep down this was all just a horrible nightmare.

*****

The serenity of the walk home that beautiful afternoon on the cobblestone walkways in Charleston contradicted her reality. In what seemed like the blink of an eye, Darcy's fairytale of being married to the man of her dreams had shattered. Her knight in shining armor was gone, and she'd never felt more scared and alone. *Where is he, Lord? Where's my precious Dillon?*

A warm hand rested on Darcy's shoulder. She paused, and Steve stepped in front of her with his hand remaining on her shoulder. "Look, I know you must have so many emotions going through your mind right now, and I'm so sorry you're going through such a horrible ordeal."

Heat rose to Darcy's cheeks in a flash on anger, and she opened her mouth to let him know exactly how she felt, but he quickly held up his index finger and she hesitated. Steve glanced at her and leveled a look at Darcy. "I sincerely hope your husband is found quickly and unharmed. I also want you to know I honestly believe my sister's a victim of this terrible guy too. I know you don't know Cindy, but she's one of the sweetest ladies I know. She'll do anything for anyone. He probably showed her attention and love. That's the only reason I can see her being with such a jerk."

Darcy maintained eye contact with Steve, unsure of what to say. The anger inside her seared like a branding iron against a bull. In her heart, she knew he was probably right, but someone must be held accountable. Darcy pursed her lips and looked heavenward, determined to control her response. "Look, she may be a victim," she said more sternly than she meant to and softened her voice as she continued. "But if it wasn't for your sister, my husband would've been home, and we wouldn't be here today having this discussion."

Steve nodded. "I can see why you'd have those feelings. If your husband's anything like I've heard you and others describe him as, he would be wherever he was needed to help anyone."

Darcy lowered her head and stared at her shoes while slowly nodding her head.

"Do you think we can both agree your husband and my sister are victims and put aside the anger so we can work together to find them? Then this sorry excuse of a man can be put behind bars for his actions."

Darcy's reserve melted, and she peered into his eyes. "You're right. I'm sorry. I'm just so worried about Dillon and just want him home," she said as tears flowed down her cheeks.

Steve blinked, patting Darcy on the shoulder as he stepped to her side. They returned to their walk. Quiet hung between them until Steve approached his hotel. "Well, this is where I'm staying. Stay strong. I'm sure your husband and my sister will be found soon. They both will be just fine, and we can get on with our lives."

At a loss for words, Darcy only nodded her head and quietly turned and continued her walk home. She stopped and looked back. "Wait!" she yelled as Steve headed toward the hotel. "How do I get in touch with you if I hear anything?" she asked. Steve returned to

Darcy and wrote down his contact information on the pad she pulled from her purse.

\*\*\*\*\*

"Hello?"

"Hey, Pastor Watson, it's Darcy."

"Hey, how did it go?"

"They really didn't have much more information than we already knew. Officer Riddle said they're trying to track down Michael's family out west. Maybe they'll locate someone who can tell us where they are and help bring Dillon home." Memories of their first year together filled her thoughts as the emptiness in her heart grew deeper and deeper. Desperate to stop her thoughts from traveling the dark, lonely path, she forced her attention to Pastor Watson on the other end of the phone. "Why don't you bring Hope home and I'll make dinner for all of us. I can fill you in on the details then."

"That sounds wonderful. Will an hour be good for you? Hope and I can pick up a dessert to bring over."

"That's perfect, Pastor Watson. I'll see you both in an hour."

\*\*\*\*\*

Steve's thoughts went back to the awful argument with his granny as he sat on the hotel bed.

"*Stevie, come on. It's time for the evening service.*"

"*I'm not going, Granny,*" he said as he turned on his television.

"*Everyone living in this house will go to church,*" she said as she switched the set off.

"*I don't like church. Jesus has never done anything for me,*" he said.

That had been the start to the worst argument he'd ever had with the precious woman who raised him and his sister. He couldn't believe his granny could be so adamant about a man she didn't know personally—a man she'd never seen, a man she chose over her grandson.

He stood with his hands on his hips, disgusted by his inability to control his temper all those years ago. He closed his eyes, took a deep breath, and reached for the phone. After several rings, his grandmother's answering machine came on.

"Hey, Granny. I'm in Charleston but haven't found Cindy yet. All I know so far is it does seem to be her and Michael the police are looking for. They're searching for any of his relatives who live out west. I think Officer Riddle said the last phone call came from Kansas City. You can call me if you know anything about his family which may help the police find him." He paused, pulled the phone away from his ear, and was tempted to hang up but changed his mind. Slowly he placed the phone back to his ear, took a deep breath, and in a faster than normal rate of speech told her how much he loved her and appreciated her forgiving him after the terrible way he treated her. Then he hung up quickly, as if he was afraid she would pick up at any moment and he would have to actually talk to her about his regrets. *Why am I still feeling horrible about our argument? She acted like nothing happened when I saw her.*

# CHAPTER 9

*Charleston, South Carolina*

"Hey Darcy, it's Officer Riddle. I have some news I'd like to share with you before we release an update to the media. Can you come to the police department in about an hour?"

"Sure, I'll change and be right there." After a moment of silence, Darcy turned toward Hope. She was laughing as the silly cat fell from the cage as he tried to get the cute yellow bird once again on the cartoon she was watching. "Hope, sweetheart, we need to get dressed. I have to meet someone who has information about my husband."

"Did they find him?" she asked. Her innocent eyes met Darcy's tear-filled gaze.

She kissed Hope's forehead and pointed toward her room. "I hope so," Darcy said as she reminded Hope to grab a sweater in case the police department was cold. Within minutes, the girls were walking out the door, hand in hand, talking as they strolled the few blocks to their destination.

*****

"Hello?"

"Hey Steve, it's Officer Riddle. I have some news I'd like to share with you before we release a media update. Can you come to the police department in about an hour?" he asked and then informed Steve he invited Darcy to the meeting also.

"Sure, I'll see you in an hour."

\*\*\*\*\*

## Oakley, Idaho

"How is he?" Michael asked as Cindy closed the door leading to the makeshift hospital room where Dillon lay.

"We really should take him to the hospital."

Michael opened the door and peered inside. "We can't take him to the hospital. Don't you understand I'll go to jail for this?" he said, agitation filling his voice.

"He'll die if we don't," she begged, her voice sharper than she intended.

Michael stood at the kitchen sink, his hands white-knuckled as he gripped the cold porcelain. He looked at Cindy and then to the door she just emerged from, his face looking many years older with the knit of his brows and worry on his face. "I'll talk to Alex when he returns from the store. We'll figure out what to do then."

\*\*\*\*\*

## Charleston, South Carolina

"Good afternoon, Darcy," Officer Riddle greeted her as he opened the door leading to the conference room at the Charleston Police Department. "Who's this little cutie?"

"Officer Riddle, this is Hope. She's staying with me for a while," she said as Hope hugged her legs, peeking around them at the tall man in the blue uniform in front of Darcy.

Officer Riddle smiled at the sight. "Please, have a seat. When Mr. Parnell arrives, we'll go over the new information."

The minutes passed like hours as she sat in the empty room waiting for information concerning her husband. Hope sat quietly in the chair beside her, lost in her thoughts.

"Are you tired?" Officer Riddle asked Darcy whose hand was covering her mouth to hide her yawn as he reentered the room with Steve.

She smiled, her cheeks turning a light shade of red. "I'm a little tired lately."

"Well, let's get on with the meeting, and you can go home to rest," Officer Riddle told her as he motioned for Steve to take the seat next to Darcy who held Hope in her lap.

"Hope, would you like to see what it looks like in a jail?" Officer Riddle asked the little girl as she clung to Darcy. She nodded as Darcy helped her stand. Officer Riddle stood and briefly left the room with Hope hot on his heels. Moments later, he returned to his seat.

"We have researched Michael's family and discovered he has an older brother who lives in Oakley, Idaho." Officer Riddle turned to face Steve. "We weren't able to contact your uncle. Do you know where in Idaho he lives?

"I'm not sure. I'd have to call my grandmother. She would know their address." No one said a word. Darcy and Officer Riddle stared at Steve. He shifted in his seat and added, "My grandmother lives in Greenville. She raised Cindy and me. Cindy's my only sibling. My parents were missionaries who were murdered in Sumter when Cindy and I were in elementary school." He paused a moment, licked his dry lips and swallowed as if trying to clear the knot in his throat. "They were killed, and the killer's never been found."

"I'm sorry, I didn't know," Officer Riddle said.

Darcy's face softened as her heart skipped a beat. *How awful to lose your parents in such a violent way and at such a young age.*

"We're in contact with the police department in Oakley. They're going to Michael's brother's house to see if they can find any sign of them." Officer Riddle stood and began pacing the floor, locking his hands behind his back. "Steve, if they find them, they'll arrest Cindy too."

"Why will she be arrested?" he asked as he stood from his chair. A scowl on his face unmasked the anger he felt inside.

"Calm down," Officer Riddle said. "If she's a victim and had no control over the disappearance of Dr. Collins, then she'll be released."

"Cindy would never hurt anyone."

"I hope you're right."

"What can we do for now?" Darcy asked.

"Just go home and rest. You'll need your strength when we find out something," he explained and turned to face Steve.

"Will you be at the Fultan Lane Inn?" Officer Riddle asked as he turned to face Steve.

"I'll probably go back to Greenville. The hotel's a little pricey for a sailor's wage," he said his voice sharp.

"I have a guest room you can rent for a couple of days while we wait for more information," Darcy volunteered; her heart skipped a beat as she realized what she offered. *I don't really know this guy. What's wrong with me?* Despite her questions, she felt a peace. She felt it was what God wanted her to do.

Steve relaxed at her kind gesture. "That would be wonderful if it wouldn't be an imposition. I can help out around the house to earn my keep."

Darcy softly smiled. "I'm going home when I leave here. You're welcome to come over this evening if you'd like."

"Are you sure I won't be putting you out?" he asked, gentleness overcoming his stoic face.

"No, I have plenty of room. Besides, you can help with some of the neglected yard work and if there's a break in the case you'll be close and can help."

"Okay then, I'll call your house, Darcy, as soon as I hear anything," Officer Riddle said as he opened to door for them to leave.

# CHAPTER 10

*Oakley, Idaho*

"Michael, have you not heard a word I said? We must leave now. The police will find out you have a brother, and this will be the first place they'll look." Michael swiveled to look at Alex who was sitting behind him.

"Yes, I heard you, but I'm not taking him to a hospital, and I'm not going to jail."

"We have to do something. We can't just sit here."

Michael's gaze drifted over the comatose man, and he was shocked at the unhealthy gray pallor of the man's cheeks.

Tension bounced between the two brothers. Michael stood and turned toward his wife. She stiffened in her seat as he stared at her. He swallowed, trying to slow his heart. Sweat trickled from his brow as he began pacing the floor, scheming to get rid of this burden.

*Lord, help us in this situation. Please change Michael's heart. Help him to do what's right,* Cindy prayed as she watched him walk the kitchen floor. She tried not to let desperation fill her, but she knew there were few options for them at this point.

"I know what we'll do," he said, his breathing rapid and his voice shaky. His brows drew together. His gaze as he looked from her to his brother filled Cindy with apprehension.

*****

## Charleston, South Carolina

"Good morning," Steve said as he awakened to a pair of sea-green eyes gazing at him.

"Are you Mrs. Darcy's husband?" the cute little girl with the dark wavy hair asked.

Steve's thoughts returned to the café where he saw this spry youngster telling her stories to Darcy, whom he thought was her mother, and the gentleman she called Pastor Watson. "No, I'm not," he answered as he pushed himself up from the pillow and leaned against the wooden headboard. "I thought you were her daughter."

"No, I'm Hope. Mrs. Darcy is taking care of me for a while," she candidly answered and hopped onto the bed. "If you aren't her husband, then who are you?"

Steve sat on the bed, intrigued by the adorable tiny chatterbox now sitting comfortably beside him.

"I think Mrs. Darcy is sick. Can you make breakfast for me?" she asked, not giving him time to answer her previous question.

"Sick?"

"Yeah, she was in her bathroom making weird noises," she answered as she jumped from the bed. "Are you coming? I'm really hungry."

He rose from the bed and followed her to the kitchen.

*****

## Oakley, Idaho

Cindy's heart squeezed inside her chest, but she managed to keep her fear from seizing her.

"Is he ready?" Michael asked as she walked by him in the kitchen. When she didn't answer, he grabbed her arm and pulled her toward him. "Is he ready?"

Chills from within burst through her body, causing a series of bumps to cover her arms and legs. Overcome with despair and disgust, Cindy cried, "You won't get away with this. If you don't take him to a hospital, he'll die, and you'll be responsible for his death."

Michael didn't bother to acknowledge her comment. "Tell Alex we're ready."

She kept her face expressionless, determined to keep peace with her now sober husband. "Where's your brother?"

"He's in the garage getting the truck ready."

*Truck, what truck?* she thought as she opened the garage door and scanned the room for the pudgy gray-haired man. *What's he doing in here? What's he doing with a truck? Where's our car?* confusion clouded her thoughts.

"What's wrong?" Alex asked, interrupting her quest for answers.

She hesitated. "Michael wanted me to let you know we're ready." Cindy's mind swirled. *Lord, please rescue us. At least save Dillon. He's done nothing but help me. Lord, is his death your answer? I don't want him to die! Please help us.*

"Give me five minutes, and you can leave," he told her, never turning from his task at hand.

*****

## Charleston, South Carolina

Darcy stood in the doorway of the kitchen, a smile pulling at the corner of her mouth as she watched the comical scene. Batter splattered on Hope and the counter as the girl continued to stir the mixture. Steve ran his hand through his hair and cracked another egg. "Take that, Mr. Egg," he said as he plopped it into the bowl. Hope giggled at his animated voice.

*Lord, I know you're with me, but right now I feel so alone. Dillon should be in this kitchen with Hope. Instead, there stands a stranger.*

*Please keep Dillon safe and bring him home soon. Protect him and show him mercy and grace.* Only God knew when or if she would see him again. She forced such thoughts from her mind, at least for the moment.

"Would you like some help?" she asked, quickly coming to Steve's rescue.

"Mrs. Darcy!" Hope yelled, running to her, awaiting arms for the hug she had grown to love and expect. Darcy bent to hug the child, but the room started spinning. Her hand covered her mouth, and she started to sway.

Steve was quickly by her side. He took Darcy by the arm and led her to the closest chair. "Here, have a seat. Are you okay?" he asked.

"Yeah, I'm just not feeling great this morning. Is something burning?" she asked as she crinkled her nose at the odor.

Steve rushed to the kitchen and returned a few moments later with the smoking pan. "I guess I'll go out and pick up breakfast since I just burned this one."

"Are you sure?" she asked. "I'm just a little tired, but I think I can manage breakfast."

"Yea, it's the least I can do since I burned the pancakes and eggs."

She smirked at the mention of the fiasco in the kitchen. "I'll be glad to make breakfast. I just need a few minutes to pull myself together."

"No, you need to rest. I'll run to the bakery and bring breakfast back shortly," he said as he turned and picked his wallet up from the table and placed it in his pocket.

"Can I go with you?" the words tumbled from Hope's mouth as she jumped up and down.

"Sure, if it's okay with Mrs. Darcy."

Darcy smiled and nodded her head, causing a piercing squeal to escape from the innocent face smiling up, pleased with her answer.

*****

Steve listened as Hope chattered on about the cartoon she watched earlier as they walked down the street toward the bakery. Steve opened the door and ushered Hope inside. "What looks good?" he asked as the two stood in front of the glass counter displaying an array of muffins and breakfast sandwiches.

"I like blueberry muffins, but Mrs. Darcy always gets the bran ones."

"Okay, then that's what we'll have," he answered and placed his order. Once the order was filled, the two left the bakery, both lost in their own thoughts.

A block from the house, Hope tilted her head to look at Steve's face. "If Mrs. Darcy's husband doesn't come back, are you going to marry her?"

Steve stared at her. "Mr. Dillon will be home. There're a lot of people looking for him."

Hope blinked up at him. "I know. Mrs. Darcy said people are praying for him too. But if he doesn't come back, will you marry Mrs. Darcy?"

"Well, it's about time you two turtles returned with breakfast," Darcy called from the porch.

Grateful for being rescued from the uncomfortable conversation, Steve looked toward the voice and smiled. "We had to wait in a long line," he explained as they climbed the steps and followed her to the kitchen where they were greeted by the wonderful smell of fresh-brewed coffee.

# CHAPTER 11

*Oakley, Idaho*

The closer she came to the garage, the faster her heart pounded, threatening to explode from the dread of what was to come. When she reached the garage, she noticed neither her husband nor his brother were there. She headed toward the truck to do as she was instructed, hoping Michael would do the right thing, but she knew better. Her hands trembled as she approached the bed of the truck. Its contents horrified her. Cindy closed her eyes and drew in a long breath, willing her racing heart to calm. As she loomed over Dillon, she fought tears ready to spill from her watery blue eyes. She bent forward, leaning on the edge of the truck, her mouth close to Dillon's ear. "Hang in there, I'm going to try to figure out a way to help you."

"Just put the supplies in the back and get in," Michael said, causing her to jump. She placed the supplies in the truck, careful to set them away from Dillon so he could be as comfortable as possible.

"We're ready to go," he said as he settled into the truck.

Michael started the vehicle and began backing down the driveway. Not wanting to be noticed leaving, he chose to leave the headlights off. It was dark on the feedlot at this early hour, making it difficult for him to stay off the grass.

"Michael, please take him to the hospital. I don't want him to die," Cindy pleaded from the passenger's seat.

"It was his choice to come to our house, so if he dies, it's his fault," he said, his alcohol-soaked breath assaulting her nose.

She closed her eyes and held her breath as she tried not to hurl. "I know he chose to come over, but I'm the one who called him. Please, honey, please take him to the hospital."

"How am I supposed to do that? I'm not going to jail," he said as they pulled out of the driveway and headed down the endless 600 West road. There were no streetlights and only the occasional light from a distant farm. Cindy knew it was pointless to discuss this issue further. She reclined as much as she could in the small truck and tried to rest.

*Lord, I know I don't deserve any blessings. I've done everything but live for you. Please, even if I don't make it, please touch Dillon and help him be reunited with his wife,* she prayed as sleep took its time claiming her.

\*\*\*\*\*

## Charleston, South Carolina

Three hours later, Steve let himself in the back door of the house, which placed him directly in the kitchen. He was hot and sweaty, and his dark hair was plastered to his forehead. It was almost noon, and the temperature in Charleston had already reached ninety-two degrees. It had been unusually hot the last few days, but Darcy's yard was in dire need of attention. With his dirt-and-grass-covered forearm, Steve wiped away the sweat trickling from his head, leaving a smudge only shades lighter than his hair. He was looking forward to a glass of cold water. The sound of crying stopped him dead in his tracks. He turned and saw Hope sitting at the kitchen table, her head lying on her arms. Not comfortable with children, Steve looked around the kitchen but didn't see Darcy. *Well, I guess it's up to me,* he thought as he sat in the chair next to the weeping little girl. "Hey squirt, what's wrong?" he asked as he placed an arm around her slumped shoulders.

"Mrs. Darcy's sick again," she said between sobs.

"She'll be okay. I'll go check on her in a moment."

"But she's sick a lot lately. I don't want her to die like my daddy did." Hope sniffled as she climbed onto his lap; she hugged her arms around his neck, oblivious to the dirt and sweat on him.

They sat together wrapped in each other's arms for the next few minutes. He kissed the top of her head, the wavy black hair tickling his nose. "I don't know what's wrong with her, but I'll go and check. I'll ask her to call her doctor. Would that help you feel better?"

She nodded as she wiped her nose on the sleeve of her dress. "Can we pray for her too?" she asked as she peered into his eyes.

"Yeah, sure," he said, unsure of what to do next. *Has someone already brainwashed this kid into believing in God?* "Okay, why don't you pray for her while I check on her? After you pray, you need to go change. Between my sweat and dirt and you wiping your nose, your dress is dirty."

Before he could leave, Hope smiled and took his hand. She closed her eyes and began her prayer. "God, Mrs. Darcy's sick and needs you. I know you are busy, but can you take a moment and make her better? I love Mrs. Darcy and want her to feel better. Amen."

After her prayer, she jumped from the chair and made a beeline for her room, Steve on her tail. Once Hope entered her room, Steve stopped at the door for only a second. "Next time you need to wipe your nose, you may want to use a tissue. I don't think Mrs. Darcy would approve of you using your sleeve."

"Yes, sir," she said as she picked another dress from her closet, waiting for Steve to help her reach it. After handing the dress to Hope, he walked to Darcy's room.

"Hey," he said softly as he entered Darcy's bedroom through the open door. Even though she didn't turn to look at him, he could tell she was weak and sick. "Hope said you've not been feeling well lately."

"I think it's just the stress of not knowing where or how Dillon is," she said as she began to weep.

"Hope's really worried, and I'm concerned too. You don't look well. Will you call your doctor?" he asked, unsure of how to help the frail body lying on the bed.

She could only nod. "Yes, I will." With that, she rose from the bed and reached for the phone on the oak table beside her bed.

Wishing to give her privacy, Steve left to check on Hope, closing the bedroom door behind him.

*****

Steve watched Hope as she wrapped her doll in the small blanket, gently singing "Amazing Grace" to the still figure in her arms. Memories of his grandmother, gently singing the same song, reminded him of the care she gave to him and his sister. Without another thought, Steve reached for the phone and dialed the all-too-familiar number. He waited, listening to each ring as it echoed in his ears.

"Hello?" answered a sweet, fragile voice.

"Hey, Granny, how are you today?"

"Stevie, I'm so glad to hear from you. I'm good. How are you, honey? Is everything all right?" she asked.

"Granny, I'm fine, but I'm worried about Cindy. I haven't found her, but it doesn't look good. The police think they went west."

"Oh no," she said, her voice trembling with fear.

"The police think Cindy's involved with the kidnapping. It's really dangerous for her to be on the run. I hope they find them soon so we can get everything straightened out," he explained.

"Do you think she had anything to do with it?"

"I honestly don't. I believe she was kidnapped too. I just hope they find them before it's too late."

"Steve, please call me and let me know if you find anything out. In the meantime, I'll pray for them."

*Praying has never helped a thing,* he thought. "You do that, Granny. I'll call you as soon as I hear anything new. By the way, can you give me any information about our relatives in Idaho? The police think they may be going in that direction." After getting the information from his grandmother, he hung up and called Officer Riddle.

# CHAPTER 12

*Oakley, Idaho*

The truck slowed and came to a stop behind a small grove of trees. Cindy awakened when she heard the door open. It was still dark and difficult for her to tell where they were. *Where are we? Why are we here?* she thought as she opened her door and exited the vehicle. "Where are we?" she asked as Michael headed away from the truck and the road.

"Don't worry about it. Just stay there," he said as he continued his search.

*What's he looking for?* she thought. She didn't have to wonder long. He returned and peered into the truck bed. "Is he still alive?" she asked as she timidly approached the bed of the truck.

"I don't know, and I really don't care. No one will ever find him when we dump him into Snake Canyon. Help me get him out of the truck and carry him to the ridge." The two removed the blue tarp from the back of the truck and spread it onto the ground.

*Lord, help us!* she pleaded, afraid they would kill Dillon. *I'm the only witness.* When that thought crossed her mind, she became terrified. She knew she had to do something to save her and Dillon. She looked back toward the truck where Michael was removing the lifeless body. He placed Dillon on the tarp and began searching the truck for rope and duct tape.

She inspected what surroundings she could see in the darkness. She noticed another grove of trees about fifty yards from the truck. Desperate to save herself, she searched the truck for the keys. *I should have known he'd take the keys,* she thought to herself. She looked back at Michael as he continued his search for the rope and tape.

Seeing her opportunity, Cindy began to run as quickly as she could toward the grove of trees. She looked back just as Michael lookup from his search. He bolted toward her. Cindy could hear his heavy footsteps closing in as she raced over uneven ground. Seconds later, Michael tackled her, and they both tumbled to the ground.

"What do you think you're doing?" he yelled just before he noticed the light from the distant farmhouse come on. "Get up. We have to get out of here before the farmer comes out."

"What about Dillon?"

"We don't have time to deal with him," he said as he dragged her to the truck, his fingers digging into her fragile, sore arm.

*****

## Charleston, South Carolina

Darcy's hand went to her mouth. "You must be mistaken. This can't be true."

"Darcy, I'm certain. I'd like to monitor your situation closely considering the extreme stress you're under right now," the doctor said as he made notes in her chart. "Make an appointment for two weeks out, and let's put together a care plan."

Darcy shook her head but couldn't speak. In her mind, his diagnosis couldn't be true. She gathered her purse and walked to the receptionist.

*****

## Oakley, Idaho
## Snake Canyon

"Who's out here? What's going on?" the farmer yelled, shotgun pointed, as he walked toward the noise he'd heard minutes ago. Not a sound could be heard. The farmer stopped when he spotted the tail-lights of a vehicle speeding down the road. *Stupid kids must be parking. I had a curfew at their age. Parents should be more responsible today and stop allowing these kids out at this time of night.* Confident all was well outside, he called for his dog. "Buck, come boy," he yelled, but the dog continued running toward the trees. *I don't know why I keep that dog. He never listens.* The old farmer fussed as he walked toward the disobedient dog. "What're you doing, boy?" he asked as he approached but froze as he saw Buck sniffing the unmoving body lying on a blue tarp.

The farmer reached for the man's neck and felt a faint pulse. "Man, hang on, I'll get help," he said to the unmoving body as he stood and rushed to his home to call 911.

*****

## Charleston, South Carolina

Steve was on the verge of getting up to start the dishes when Darcy entered the living room. She looked stricken as she sat on the sofa and stared at the wall. "Are you okay?" he finally managed to ask.

Hope stood in the hallway, unnoticed by either adult.

Darcy slowly turned to Steve and said, "I'm pregnant."

Squeals of delight filled the room as Hope ran to Darcy, jumped into her lap, and threw her arms around Darcy's neck. Darcy sank into the sofa as she relished the hug from the happy little girl, a hug she should be sharing with her husband.

Steve's heart broke as he saw the pain and fear in Darcy's eyes. "I'll help you in any way I can. At least until Dillon comes home."

*Dillon,* she thought. *He would be so happy. He wanted a baby since the day we married. Why, Lord! Why is this happening? I'm only twenty-three. Twenty-three, pregnant, and no husband. Where's my hus-band?* she yelled silently as she closed her eyes. Tears trickled down her face as she held onto Hope. *It's not fair. Life just isn't fair. I pray and pray, and it seems You're not listening.*

# CHAPTER 13

*Oakley, Idaho*

*Snake Canyon*

"Oh, man, this guy's in really rough shape. Do you feel a pulse?" the paramedic asked his partner who was working on the limp body lying on the tarp.

"It's very faint. We need to get him to the hospital quick. Go call for a helicopter." The first paramedic ran toward the ambulance to radio for help. "Hold on, man. We're going to help you," the kneeling paramedic said to the unconscious man in front of him while searching his pockets for identification.

"They're sending the helicopter," his partner said as here turned. "Were you able to find out who he is?"

"No, there's no identification. Whoever he is, he's really suffered. I've never seen anyone beaten so badly." The two men stood there, staring at the beaten man.

The sound of sirens snapped them from their shocked state. "Looks like the police are here."

"Yeah, and the helicopter should be here soon."

"Gentleman, what do we have here?" the officer asked as he approached the paramedics.

"We don't know who he is. There's no identification. He's been severely beaten and has a faint pulse," the paramedic in charge told the officer.

"Is he stable enough to transport?" the officer yelled over the sound of the helicopter landing nearby.

"He's as stable as we can get him out here. He really should've been in the hospital long ago. I just hope it's not too late."

# CHAPTER 14

*Oakley, Idaho*

"Where are we going?" Cindy asked after hours of silence. "Just shut up. I don't know where we're going or what we're going to do. I don't know why I ever married you. You're the stupidest woman I know. Now they'll find that doctor, and we'll go to jail. This is all your fault! If you'd stayed in the truck like I told you to, we wouldn't be in this position."

Afraid to say anything further, Cindy sat back, closed her eyes, and prayed.

*****

*My name is Dillon Collins!* he yelled over and over but not a sound was heard. *Why aren't you listening to me? Ouch! That hurts. Stop sticking me. What's going on?* Moments later, he felt his world begin to spin, and he surrendered to the peaceful, pain-free sleep induced by the morphine pumped into his arm.

"We'll keep him sedated until some of the internal wounds heal. Maybe someone will come and identify him. Poor guy looks like someone ran over him with a truck," the doctor said as he handed the nurse the chart.

"What are his chances of pulling through?" she asked as she took the chart and placed it on the foot of the bed.

"Well, the next few days will be critical. If he makes it through the next twenty-four hours, his chances will improve. It'd really help if he had family here to talk to him and encourage him," the doctor said as he left the room.

# CHAPTER 15

Michael knew his life would never be the same. He had no idea where to go or what to do. With no destination in mind, he drove aimlessly, too scared to stop. *Why did I ever hurt her? What've I done? Why do I continue to drink?* Hungry and tired, he followed the signs to Pocatello and pulled into a rundown hotel, seeking rest. "Get out and come with me. If you try anything, you'll regret it. Do you understand?"

She nodded and did as she was ordered, her hands shaking and eyes wide.

*****

He could hear voices but couldn't make them out. Pain seared through his body, and he wanted to scream, but he couldn't make a sound. More voices, female voices. *Were they talking to me?*

"Does anyone know who he is yet?" the doctor asked as he entered the room.

"No. It's been twenty-four hours, and the police still haven't received a missing person's report."

"How sad, I wish we could find his family."

*My name is Dillon. Why won't you listen to me?* he screamed only for himself to hear. *What's that?* he wondered at the stinging in his arm again. Soon, he drifted into the sweet world of dreams—dreams of Darcy, their wedding day, working at the hospital, and arriving home to the wonderful aroma of fresh-baked bread.

*****

*Pocatello, Idaho*

Michael unlocked the door, and the tired travelers entered the small musky-smelling room. "Go shower, and I'll get some us food," he said as he pointed toward the bathroom.

Cindy didn't say a word. She just walked to the bathroom, shut the door, and turned the water on. She stood quietly in the bathroom, listening for her husband to leave. The door creaked open and slammed shut. Confident he was gone, she walked out of the bathroom.

"Where are you going?" he asked, looking into the shocked face of his wife.

"I was just coming out to look for something clean to wear," she explained, trying not to let the fear in her voice give her away. "I was hoping someone left something behind. My clothes are dirty and bloody, and I'd like to change."

"Go shower, you'll have to make do with what you have."

She walked back to the shower, undressed, and let the warm water drench her body. She was grateful she was in the shower because seconds later, the shower curtain flung open to make sure she was doing as she was told.

Satisfied she would stay put this time, he left in search of food.

# CHAPTER 16

*Charleston, South Carolina*

Darcy lay looking at the ceiling as she listened to Steve and Hope playing in the living room. The gentle way Steve played with Hope brought tears to her eyes. *Dillon, I miss you so much. Where are you? Why haven't you called?* Knowing if she stayed in bed she would continue to cry, she got up and dressed. She pushed the thoughts of Dillon from her mind. She was brushing her hair when the phone rang. "Hello?"

"May I speak with Darcy?"

"This is Darcy."

"Hey, Darcy, this is Officer Riddle. I just wanted to bring you up-to-date on our investigation."

"Have you found my husband?" she asked and was so caught up in her conversation, she didn't hear Steve and Hope enter the room. After a few moments, she returned the phone to the cradle and closed her eyes to pray, still unaware of the two watching her from the door.

"Are you okay?" Hope asked as Darcy opened her eyes.

Darcy nodded as she looked at the dark eyes staring at her. "Yes, honey. I was just praying. The police in Idaho are following a lead, which may lead to finding my husband."

That was enough information for Hope, who ran off to play.

Steve scratched the back of his head. "Did they say where in Idaho?"

"No, he just said they were following a lead."

Steve was quiet for a while. *What if the police are wrong, and they did go to the Sanders?* he wondered. *Is Cindy involved in this?*

Not knowing what to say, Darcy mumbled something about going to the store and made a hasty exit, leaving Hope in Steve's care.

*****

## Oakley, Idaho

The officers drove down the gravel drive to the silvery-gray double-wide and parked next to the wooden sign directing them to the office. "Well, it looks like the office to Bedke Feedlot is at the rear of this double-wide," the officer driving the car said as he opened the car door.

"My goodness," the other officer, a wiry man of about sixty with thinning white hair said. "How do these people work in this? The stench is horrible," he grunted as he exited the vehicle to the sound of cows mooing and the smell of manure.

"I guess you get used to it. I don't know if I could, it is pretty rough," the first officer said as he led the way to the rear door toward the white plastic sign with black lettering that read OPEN. He grasped the plastic handle of the door and pulled. "Well, the sign says they are open, but this door is locked. I'll walk around and see if I can find someone."

"Okay, I'll wait here in case they come in," the second officer said as he sat on the bench along the walkway.

The next ten minutes were peaceful except for the occasional *moo* by one of the thousands of cows in the pens about one hundred yards behind him. The porch and shutters were in dire need of painting. *How in the world do they work with this smell?* The older officer wondered as the younger officer returned with a beastly man who looked to be in his sixties but towered the younger officer. As the men approached, the older officer stood, staring at the burly man beside his partner.

"Harley Sanders!" the older officer said with a smile in his eyes. "How in the world have you been?"

The face before him was thin, his cheeks nearly sunken. Time had not been kind to his old friend. "John, how are you?"

"I've had some medical problems, but I'm bouncing back. How about you? I haven't seen you in years. I didn't know you owned Bedke Feedlot."

"I don't. I sold my feedlot to my daughter and her husband. I just piddle around trying to stay busy."

"Well, you look great!" John said as he turned toward his partner, as if he just remembered the younger officer standing at his side. "I'm sorry. Curtis, this is a dear friend of mine, Harley Sanders. Harley, this is my new partner, Curtis Grant."

"It's a pleasure to meet you, Mr. Sanders."

"Please, call me Harley. Gentlemen, come on in," Harley said as he unlocked the door and led the men to the very informal office just off the kitchen in the home.

The men sat on the sofa against the wall facing the desk. They all listened as John filled Harley in on what they were looking for. Harley nodded silently as a confused, troubled expression came across his face. He opened his mouth to speak, but his wife, Garrell entered the room with coffee for everyone.

Harley was shocked and dumbfounded. He never expected to receive such news about one of his best employees and wondered if the officers had the right man.

"Well, I hope you're wrong," Harley said as he stood and led the men outside. "Alex is one of my best employees and has been with us for years. He's like one of the family. He lives in the last mobile home on the left. The one with the garage beside it, located just past the cow pens. You're welcome to look around."

"Thanks, Harley. I hope we're wrong too."

The officers returned to their car and drove around the cow pens to the row of homes at the back of the property.

# CHAPTER 17

*Pocatello, Idaho*

She rushed from the shower, dried as fast as she could, and threw on her filthy clothing. Her eyes scanned the room as she emerged from the bathroom in search of her husband. Satisfied he was still away, she eased open the door to see if she could make it to the office before he returned. She closed the door and dropped to the bed, scared to leave the room, tears dropping from her eyes as she tried to figure out what to do next. *How can anyone think with all the noise from those kids playing?* It was then the idea hit her. She scribbled a note on the pad beside the phone, opened the door, and called toward the children. "Excuse me, can one of you guys help me?" she asked as the children stopped their game of basketball and looked at the cruddy woman. "Please," she pleaded.

Two of the bigger boys cautiously approached her. When they were near the room, she stuck her hand out, revealing the note. "I need someone to take this to the office. It's important. Would you please help me?"

The boys looked at each other and then at the note. "Sure, lady," the taller of the two said as he took the note from her. The boys ran toward the office, and Cindy closed the door with a sigh of relief and a feeling of hope she hadn't felt in a long while. *Now maybe Dillon will get some help.* No sooner than the thought crossed her mind, the door flung open, and there was Michael. His arms filled with bags of food and drinks.

"What are those brats doing around this room?" he asked, staring at his wife.

"I don't know. I just got out of the shower. I guess they're playing," she answered as she drew a deep breath and took the bags from him, careful not to look him in the eyes.

She sat the food on the dresser and began preparing their sandwiches.

After they finished eating the sandwiches, Michael kicked off his shoes. "I'm going to get some sleep now, and then we have to hit the road again," he said as he reached into his duffle bag and removed some rope. "Get over here."

Cindy hesitated when she saw the rope. "Michael, you don't have to do that. I don't know where we are, and even if I did, I'm not going anywhere. I love you." Her plea fell on deaf ears.

"Get over here!" he yelled.

When she approached her husband, he grabbed her by the arm, pushed her to the bed, and tied her hands to the headboard. "Now, I'll be able to sleep." Minutes later, Cindy lay there listening to the sound of his snores, tears streaming down her face.

*****

"I received this note from a kid who states a woman staying in one of our rooms gave it to him. I thought you may be interested in it," the clerk said as she handed the folded note to the officer.

He unfolded the paper she handed him and stood frozen as he reread the note. "Wow, I'll call for back up. If this is true, we may be in for a fight." He took the note and headed toward his car. "Dispatch, this is Bravo 54 and we need a 10-33 at the Red Lion Hotel for a possible kidnapping and assault from South Carolina."

"Ten-four, Bravo 54, assistance is on the way."

The officer returned to the office of the hotel. "Which room are they in?"

"They're in room 113. I haven't seen them since they checked in."

"Do you remember what they're driving?"

"I think it was the little red truck parked in front of the ice machine."

"Thanks, I'm going to wait outside for backup so I can watch the room. Is there any other way out except the front door?"

"No, that's the only door."

"Thank you. Stay inside, and if you don't mind, if anyone comes in, ask them to stay here until we can resolve this situation."

"Okay."

*****

## Oakley, Idaho

The police department was in a small brick building in the center of town. The lobby was bare except for six folding chairs sitting against the unadorned beige block wall. The officers walked through the lobby and straight to the chief's office. They knocked on his door and waited for an answer.

"Come in."

The two officers entered the room, closing the door behind them. The chief motioned for them to sit in the two leather chairs across from his desk. He was a big man in his midsixties, and his size made the office appear small. He was fiddling with some files, so the men waited until they had his full attention.

"Well, are you two going to tell me what happened or just sit there like knots on a log?" he asked as he tossed the files on top of the stack already on the floor beside the desk.

"We talked with Alex Hogan, but he said he hasn't seen his brother in years. We went to the Bedke Feedlot and talked with the owner a Mr.—," Curtis said as he flipped through his notes to find the name.

"Mr. Harley Sanders," John said.

"Harley and Garrell Sanders?" the chief asked.

"Yes, sir, do you know them?" John asked, amused the chief knew their names.

"Sure, I know Harley and Garrell. They're good friends of mine."

"What a small world. I know them too. Harley and I were friends in the military. I haven't seen him in years until today."

"Enough small talk," the chief said, his tone now serious. "What did you find out when you talked with Alex?"

"Well, sir, we didn't find out a lot. He does work at the Bedke Feedlot and lives in one of the mobile homes provided for the workers. He claims he doesn't know where his brother lives nor has any contact information for his brother. However, when we walked the property, we did see a blue Monarch with a South Carolina tag. When we ran the tag, it came back to a Cindy Hogan from Charleston, South Carolina," Curtis told the chief.

"Okay, I'll call the Charleston Police Department and let them know the progress so far. Why don't you two get a search warrant and search Mr. Hogan's home and especially that car."

Without another word, the two officers rose from their chairs and left the office.

# CHAPTER 18

*Oakley, Idaho*

"How's our patient?" the nurse asked as she walked into the room to check the unknown man's vital signs.

"I'm afraid he's not doing well at all. He's running a fever. We need to perform surgery on his leg, but it's too dangerous to operate while he's so unstable. I wish we could find out who he is so we could contact his family. Sometimes a patient heals quicker just having family close by," the doctor said as he handed the nurse the chart he just finished with.

"The police department said they would call us as soon as they were able to identify him. It seems like someone would have reported him missing by now."

The doctor nodded. "Keep him on pain medication so his body can heal. I also prescribed some antibiotics for the infection which should help with the fever. Call me if there are any changes."

"Yes, sir," the nurse said as she continued her examination.

\*\*\*\*\*

## *Charleston, South Carolina*

Darcy and Steve strolled along the shore's edge while Hope ran back and forth in front of them, daring the waves to catch her. "Darcy, I'm sure the police will find Dillon, and he'll be okay. Please don't cry. He'll be home before you know it, helping you raise Hope and the little one you're carrying."

"I hope you're right. I don't know what I'll do if he doesn't return. He would be so excited about the baby. We decided from the first day of our marriage that we wanted to have children. We always dreamed of having a houseful running around."

Steve Parnell wasn't the sort of man who was comfortable dealing with emotions. Not knowing what else to say, he elected to remain quiet. The wind was warm against his face, and the water lapped at his feet. He was content with the quiet until he heard the soft sound of crying. His heart melted when he looked at Darcy and saw the anguish and fear covering her smooth features. He started to speak, but at that moment, Hope ran to them to share the treasure she found on the beach.

"Look, a clam," she exclaimed as she held the closed shell in the palm of her hand for them to see.

"What a neat treasure," Darcy said as she sat on the sand to better examine the little girl's find. "Do you know what clams do?"

Hope screwed up her mouth and closed her eyes. Darcy looked toward Steve and smiled as they watched her try to figure out what a clam does. "It lives in the sea," she said after a few minutes of contemplation.

"Yes, they do, but did you know a clam makes pearls?" Darcy asked as Hope scooted closer to her.

Hope's eyes grew large with this new information. "How do they make pearls?"

"The clam gets sand in its shell, and the sand irritates the clam. The clam then turns the irritation into something beautiful. That's how they make the pearl."

"Wow!" She glanced at the clam in her tiny hands and gently laid it on the sand.

Darcy continued while she had the little girl's attention. "See, God wants us to be like clams."

"He wants us to live in the sea?"

"No, sweetie," Darcy said with a laugh in her voice as she rose and patted Hope's mop of curls. "He wants us to take things in life that irritate us and turn them into something beautiful."

"Is that what you are doing while Mr. Dillon's gone?" Hope asked as she stood and took Darcy by the hand.

Darcy looked out at the ocean and watched the waves crash into the shore. Tears filled her eyes as she fought the knot in her throat, which was keeping her from speaking.

Seeing she needed some time, Steve rescued her by distracting Hope. "How would you like some ice cream?"

"Yes," Hope squealed and ran to his arms. He hoisted her up and walked toward the ice cream stand, leaving Darcy alone with her thoughts.

*****

## Pocatello, Idaho

"What's going on?" the officer asked as he emerged from his car.

"The clerk said a boy brought this note to her. The boy told her a lady in room 113 handed it to him. After the clerk read it, she thought she should call us."

"Have you seen them?" Officer Hiott asked.

"No, I haven't seen anyone come or go from the room. I don't know if this note is real or a prank, but with its contents, I didn't want to take any chances," he explained as he handed the note to his partner.

Please help me. I'm being held against my will by my husband. He may have also killed a man from South Carolina.

Officer Hiott reread the note to make sure he read it correctly. "Have you heard anything about a murder?"

"No, but I did hear about a man who was found near Snake Canyon last night. He was badly beaten and had no identification. The station is calling South Carolina to see if they have anyone reported missing recently, but we haven't heard back from them yet."

"Bravo 54, do you copy?" the radio squawked, interrupting the officers' conversation.

"Go ahead," Officer Hiott said as he squeezed the black button on the microphone.

"We have information concerning your inquiry. It seems there are three people missing from South Carolina. A Michael and Cindy Hogan and a Dr. Dillon Collins. It's believed Dr. Collins may be injured because his blood was found in the Hogans' home."

"Ten-four, dispatch, can we get a search warrant out here immediately? I believe they may be in a room here."

"Ten-four, we'll have one delivered to you."

"Ten-four. I'm going to contact the occupants in the room and see if they'll talk with me."

*****

## Charleston, South Carolina

Darcy's stomach was aflutter as she sat staring into the rolling sea. Realizing she was alone, Darcy stood, scanning the beach for Hope and Steve. The ringing of the phone halted her search for them. "Hello?"

"Hello Darcy, it's Officer Riddle. I need for you to come to the station. We have some news about the Hogans and Dillon. How soon can you get here?"

"I'm at the beach right now, but we'll head your way," she said as she hung up the phone and resumed her search for Steve and Hope. It wasn't long before she spotted them at the ice cream stand. She ran toward them.

Steve stood as he saw Darcy running toward them. Sensing something was wrong, he threw the remainder of his ice cream away and started cleaning Hope's hands and face. As he finished his job, Darcy reached the pair.

Breathlessly she said, "We need to go to the police station. They have some news for us."

Steve picked up Hope, and the three of them headed toward the car.

# CHAPTER 19

*Oakley, Idaho*

The officer stopped a few feet from the door. He motioned for his partner to head toward the back to make sure no one left. Once the men were in place, the officer banged on the dingy white door. "Oakley Police, open up."

The officers were greeted with a pair of mud-brown eyes, which peered at them through the tiny opening. "What do you want?" Alex asked in a gruff voice.

"We have a search warrant for your home and all other property located at this address," the officer said as he pushed open the door, causing the man to take a step back and allow the officers into his home.

"What are you searching for?"

The head officer didn't answer his question. He just handed him the warrant and entered the home. The officers began their search as Alex Hogan stayed on their heels, watching their every move.

"What are you looking for?" he asked once again.

"We know your brother's been here, and we know you helped him. If you know anything about his whereabouts, you need to tell us now, or you'll be arrested too."

Alex turned his gaze from the officers to the garage where his brother's car was hidden. *Why didn't I just turn him away? What have*

*I done? I hope that man is still alive, not just for my brother's sake but for mine too.* He had more questions but forced himself to turn his attention back to the officers still searching his home. It wouldn't do for him to go to jail and leave the Sanders without their lead man. "Officer," Alex said as he stopped by the door leading to the garage. "Would you gentlemen please have a seat? There're some things I need to tell you."

Stunned by his change in attitude, the officers complied with his request and sat at the round wooden table in the tiny kitchen.

With everyone sitting at the table, it didn't take long for Alex to tell the officers all that transpired with his brother. "They arrived around 2:00 a.m. a few days ago. There was Michael, Cindy, and another man who was badly injured. I had a doctor friend look at the man, and the doctor told my brother the man needed immediate medical attention. Michael didn't want to use the car he came in. He was afraid the police would be looking for it. I let him use my truck. They left the next morning, and I haven't seen or heard from them since."

"We need the tag and identification number on the truck and need to look at the car they arrived in for evidence," the older officer stated as they stood to continue their investigation. Alex led them to the garage where the blue Monarch sat. While the officers searched the car, Alex left to search for the tax receipt with the truck's information.

After he found the tax receipt, Alex returned to the kitchen. He sat at the kitchen table, his hands folded as he prayed, asking for protection over the injured man, protection over his brother and his brother's wife, but mostly asking for forgiveness. He prayed for forgiveness for not doing the right thing all along. The officers came into the kitchen from the garage just as Alex was completing his prayer.

"Mr. Hogan, you're not allowed to leave this city until we complete our investigation. Currently, we're not charging you with aiding and abetting. However, I need to talk with our sergeant to find out if you're going to be charged. You better hope we find them and Dr. Dillon is okay. If he dies, you could be charged as an accessory."

"Yes, sir. I understand. I'll call you if I hear from Michael," Alex said as the officers walked toward the front door.

*****

## Charleston, South Carolina

"Hello, Steve, Darcy," Officer Riddle greeted them with a raised eyebrow, a little surprised they were together since he didn't call Steve. He stepped aside and they entered his office. "Please, have a seat."

"Hope, we have a room where you can color. Would you like to go and color a picture?" Officer Riddle asked.

Hope looked at Steve and then Darcy. When both nodded their heads, she leaped from Steve's lap and was led from the room by Officer Riddle's partner.

Once Hope was out of the room, Officer Riddle sat in the leather chair across from Steve and Darcy.

Darcy felt light-headed, her stomach twisted in knots. Steve touched her arm. "Darcy, no matter what Officer Riddle has to say, I'll be here for you, for you and for Hope."

She didn't know why, but she felt comforted and safe at his touch.

Officer Riddle cleared his throat. "I've received a call from the Oakley Police Department since I talked with you earlier today. We suspected Michael would head to Idaho, and now we know he was there. The police have talked to his brother, Alex Hogan. Alex told them everything he knew."

"Did they say anything about Dillon?" Darcy asked. "You said Michael was there. Does that mean he's no longer there?" Questions flowed from her mouth as she sat slightly slumped in the chair.

Officer Riddle sat back against his chair. "Darcy, we haven't found them yet. The police went to Michael's brother's home, but Michael left before we could locate them. We do know they're driving a red truck, and the police department has the tag number. They're searching for them now."

"I understand they didn't find them, but did Alex say anything about Dillon?" she snapped. Something tightened in her chest as she tried to read the expression on Officer Riddle's face. "Officer Riddle, what do you know about my husband?" she asked again.

After what seemed like a lifetime but was, in fact, a matter of seconds, Officer Riddle began to speak, "Darcy, no one knows where he is, but they do know he was hurt. They said Alex had a doctor look at him, but they didn't take him to the hospital."

"Darcy," Steve whispered.

Darcy looked up, let out a small cry, and covered her face with her hands. The gentlemen exchanged looks, unsure of what to do. Steve stood and moved beside her, placing his arm around her shoulders, which were shaking with each sob. "It's going to be all right," he said, trying to comfort her.

Darcy looked at him with fear-filled eyes. "What if he dies?"

"Oh, Darcy," he said as he hugged her a little tighter. "He's not going to die. You'll see."

"I'm scared. Really scared," she said as she began to sob again.

"Shh," he spoke softly, trying to comfort her. "It's all right. Everything will be okay. Your God will take care of him."

Steve looked toward Officer Riddle who only nodded. "Darcy, let's go to your house so you can rest. You need to think about you and the baby right now. Dillon will be okay." With his hand on Darcy's back, he steered her toward the door.

*Baby?* Officer Riddle thought as the last comment Steve made registered in his mind. *Lord, please be with Darcy. Cover her with Your comfort and grace. Help us find Dillon, not only for her but for their unborn child.*

*****

## Pocatello, Idaho

Michael and Cindy were still asleep when they heard the deafening *boom* of the battering ram pounding on the front door of the hotel. "Police!" was all they heard as they opened their eyes to guns pointed at them from every direction.

With no time to respond, Michael lifted his hands above his head to surrender to the armed men.

"Michael Hogan, we have a warrant for your arrest," the officer stated as he approached the stunned man. The cold steel bracelets snapped as the officer secured Michael's hands behind his back. "Michael Hogan, you have the right to remain silent. Anything you say may be used against you in a court of law," the officer continued but the words were lost on Cindy who was still tied to the bed.

*Lord, what have I done?* she prayed as the officer finished with her husband and took him away. Once Michael was out of the room, the officer in charge turned toward Cindy as another officer untied her. "Cindy Hogan, you'll need to go with us to the police department until we can determine what happened."

She moved her arms in slow circles trying to relieve the tight, sore muscles. She didn't answer the officers; she rose from the bed and allowed them to escort her to the waiting police car.

Michael and Cindy were placed in separate cars for the ride to the police department. Neither spoke on the ten-minute ride.

# CHAPTER 20

*Pocatello, Idaho*

"Where's my wife?" Michael asked a bit gruffly.

"You have more to worry about than your wife," the detective said as he took the seat directly across from Michael in the small room. "We have an extradition order from Charleston where you'll face charges. Now where is Dr. Collins?" he asked as he rose from the chair and paced in front of the scrappy looking man sitting at the table.

"Charges, what charges?" A bitter laugh echoed throughout the room as Michael ignored the last question. "They ain't got nuttin' on me. No witnesses and no proof."

"Mr. Hogan, a doctor is missing, and his blood was found in the living room of your home," the officer explained as he turned to walk toward the door. "We entered the hotel room and found your wife tied to the bed and covered with—" He whirled around at the sound of a loud crash. Shards of glass from the two-way mirror covered the floor, and the wooden chair Mr. Hogan was sitting in moments ago lay against the wall and broken glass.

Michael stood with his hands on the table, heaving. "You're gonna be sorry! You don't know who you're messing with!" he yelled as four officers rushed in and wrestled him to the ground, securing him with handcuffs. He let out a string of despicable curse words before being dragged to a holding cell.

*****

"Mrs. Hogan, if you don't cooperate, you'll be charged as an accessory and probably aiding and abetting," the officer explained as he sat across the table from her.

Cindy stared at him, tears streaming from her eyes. "You don't understand. I can't testify against him. He'll kill me, and besides," she said and paused, swallowing the knot threatening to choke her, "I love him. I can't send him away."

Surprisingly, he felt compassion for her, and his tone was kinder. "I understand your fear. Cindy, you aren't sending him away. If you're a victim in this too, he did it to himself. I assure you if you testify, we'll prosecute him, and you'll be safe. He'll appear before the judge in the morning, and I'm confident with all the charges, the judge will deny him bond. If bond is denied, he'll have to stay in jail until his trial and won't be able to get to you."

His kindness hit hard, and tears continued to flow down her cheeks. She pressed the palms of her hands against her eyes and lowered her head as she sobbed. "I can't. I can't testify. If the judge allows bail, he'll kill me."

The officer huffed and turned toward the door. "Take her to her cell," he told the officer waiting by the door as he left the room. He walked toward the front desk and turned, facing the woman sitting at the desk. "Will you please call Charleston and arrange to have both of them transferred to face charges?" The woman immediately picked up the phone receiver, dialing the number as the officer walked down the hall.

# CHAPTER 21

*Charleston, South Carolina*
*Two days later*

"Mr. Michael Hogan," the judge began as he scanned the paperwork before him. "You're being charged with two counts of assault and battery with intent to kill and two counts of kidnapping." He paused and leaned into the high-back leather chair, his eyes fixed on the man in the orange jumpsuit standing before him. For some minutes, the courtroom was silent. "Do you understand these charges?"

"Yeah," Michael answered, keeping his eyes glued to the table in front of him.

"You have the right to have an attorney present and to prepare a defense. If you cannot afford an attorney, the court will appoint one for you. Do you understand these rights?"

Michael raised his head just moments later. He stood, staring at the massive wooden desk before him. Before answering the judge, he scanned the room and saw no sign of his wife. "I haven't done anything, so I don't need your lawyers," he answered, his jaw set and his eyes glaring at the judge.

"Very well," the judge said. "Since he has already proven himself to be a flight risk, bail is denied." He looked toward the deputy and said, "Take him to his cell and bring in the next defendant." The judge watched as the arrogant man was led away.

*****

Cindy studied the judge's face as she stood before him, her hands cuffed behind her back, the yellow-and-purple bruises telling him what she would not. "Are you all right?" He felt the need to ask before proceeding with her charges.

"Yes, sir," she answered as she lowered her head.

"Mrs. Hogan, you're being charged with accessory to assault and battery and kidnapping. Do you understand these charges?"

"Yes, sir."

"As I told your husband, you have the right to an attorney, if you cannot afford one, we'll appoint one for you. Would you like for the court to appoint an attorney for you?" he asked as he gazed at the battered woman before him. She could not speak or look him in the eyes; she only nodded. "Very well, the officer will take you to an office and you can fill out the appropriate paperwork. You should have an attorney in a few days. I am setting bail at ten thousand dollars," he told her as he nodded for the officer to take her away.

*****

The room Cindy was led to was small. There was a wooden table and four chairs. She was ushered to a chair directly in front of the gentleman who was introduced to her as her attorney.

"Mrs. Hogan, the district attorney has advised me if you tell the truth about what happened to you and Dr. Collins, he'll drop the charges against you and provide you with protection."

Cindy felt the blood drain from her face and was unable to respond to his statement. "Mrs. Hogan, a man's life is in danger. You can save yourself and Dr. Collins by telling us exactly what transpired and where Dr. Collins was last seen."

Cindy looked around the room and wondered where her husband was. A moment later, she found the courage to speak. "He'll kill me if I say anything."

"Mrs. Hogan, he's been denied bail and refuses an attorney. He'll stay in jail until his trial. If he's convicted of the charges, he'll face at least twenty years before he'll even have a chance at parole."

Still unsure if she should say anything, Cindy sat in silence.

"Mrs. Hogan, we know Dr. Collins was hurt. If we don't find him and he dies, you'll be charged as an accessory to murder and will face at least twenty years too."

Cindy looked at the attorney and knew what she must do. *Was this really happening?* It felt like a nightmare she couldn't wake from. She opened her mouth to speak, fighting the queasy feeling in the pit of her stomach. "Michael came home after drinking with some friends...," she continued as the attorney took notes of every detail. Her story went on for over an hour. "When he left the truck, I knew it was my chance to get away. I tried to run, but he caught me. A light came on at a house close by. Then Michael threw me into the truck and took off. Dr. Collins was left on the side of the road near a cliff."

The officer standing at the back of the room opened the door and motioned for another officer. Cindy sat quietly as the first officer stepped outside the room to speak with the approaching officer.

\*\*\*\*\*

Darcy sat on the paper-lined table, dressed in a pink paper shirt, while she waited for the doctor. A moment later, she rose from the table and began searching her purse for a piece of gum. She was nervous and needed something to keep her busy. After popping the gum into her mouth, she returned to the table just as the doctor opened the door.

"Good afternoon, Darcy," he greeted as he extended his hand to shake hers. Darcy smiled as he took a seat on the stool beside the table. "How do you feel today?"

"I'm okay. I still feel queasy in the mornings, but the rest of the day is good," she said as she placed her hand on the slight swell of her belly.

"All of the bloodwork came back okay, but I'm a little worried about your blood pressure. It's a little high," he explained, pausing to read her chart.

*Lord, please let the baby be okay. Please don't take my baby away.* Darcy suddenly stopped praying. She had many questions for the doctor. "Is the baby going to be all right?"

"Darcy, the baby's fine. Your body is under a great deal of stress right now, so it's important you rest as much as you can. You're only fifteen weeks along, so it's critical you take good care of yourself."

She sat at the end of the table and stared at the doctor. His words unheard except *your baby's fine.* "Darcy, did you hear what I said?" he asked.

Darcy shook her head.

Smiling warmly, he repeated his instructions. "I want you to go home to complete bed rest, and I'll see you back in two weeks."

"Complete bed rest?" she asked as comprehension of his orders sank in. "I can't stay in bed. I have a little girl I'm responsible for. She can't take care of herself."

"Darcy, you have no choice. If you don't, you could lose your baby or endanger your life," he clarified as he stood to go to his next appointment. "Make an appointment with the receptionist for two weeks from now. Don't hesitate to call me if you have any problems before then."

Darcy stood, got dressed, gathered her belongings, and started toward the door. Her doctor was standing in the hallway at the door leading to his next appointment.

"Darcy, I'll be praying for you. I hope you find your husband soon. Dillon is a wonderful man," he said as she smiled and nodded her thanks.

# CHAPTER 22

*Charleston, South Carolina*

C indy sat at the wooden table, staring at the cement wall in front of her. The empty room echoed the emptiness she felt inside. *Lord, I've really made a mess of my life. I remember my granny telling me no matter what someone does, You still love them even though You hate their deed. I've really messed up this time. Lord, please forgive me and give me the strength to handle whatever is to come.* She straightened in the chair and turned toward the door. Her attorney entered the room and took off his jacket, placing it across the chair in front of her. She took a deep breath and watched him with her tired, tear-filled blue eyes.

"Mrs. Parnell, an officer is going to come in here in a moment and record your statement. The police are searching the area you described in an effort to find Dr. Collins. Once your statement is taken, I'll start the process to have you released. The district attorney has agreed not to press charges since you're fully cooperating with the prosecution."

The attorney's instructions were interrupted by a rap at the door. As soon as the rap stopped, the door opened, and an officer entered the small concrete room carrying a recorder. Cindy and her attorney watched the officer as he wordlessly walked to the chair directly in front of Cindy. He placed the recorder in the center of the table and pressed two black buttons. The tape in the recorder began to turn. It was then the officer spoke. "Hello, Mrs. Hogan. My name is Officer Myers. I have been assigned to take your statement. If you will, please begin by stating your name, date of birth, and then your statement." His instructions were very mechanical, and seconds passed before Cindy realized she was supposed to speak.

Cindy turned wide eyes toward her attorney. He nodded, giving her the permission, she sought to begin. "My name is Cindy Hogan," she said and continued her account over the next couple of hours.

*****

## Boise, Idaho

Chief Teague entered the double doors of the Magic Valley Regional Medical Center and walked toward the large wooden desk located to the right of the entrance. "Hello," he said as he approached the woman sitting at the desk. "I'm Chief Teague with the Oakley Police Department. I need to see someone regarding an unidentified man who was brought in a few days ago."

Without speaking to Chief Teague, the woman behind the desk picked up her phone and dialed several numbers. "There's an officer here from the Oakley Police Department wanting to talk with someone regarding the John Doe brought in the other day." Without another word, she returned the receiver to the cradle and looked at the man standing before her. "You can have a seat. Someone will be with you shortly."

Chief Teague walked toward the blue cloth couches and picked up a magazine as he took a seat. A few minutes passed before a short gray-haired man in a white lab coat approached him.

"Hello, I'm the doctor taking care of the unidentified man. How can I help you?" he asked as the men shook hands.

"We're investigating a kidnapping from South Carolina and have reason to believe this man may be the missing doctor we're looking for."

"I hope he is. He's been in a coma since he was brought in, and people usually progress quicker when they have loved ones around," the doctor said. "Follow me, and I'll show you to his room."

The chief followed the doctor down the long white hallway.

*****

## Charleston, South Carolina

"Mrs. Darcy's home!" Hope yelled as she watched Darcy's car pull into the driveway.

Steve rose from the floor, careful not to disturb their chutes-and-ladders game and walked to the front door. He opened it as Darcy approached the porch. The lack of color on her face scared Steve. "Darcy, are you okay?" he asked as he helped her to the sofa.

"Hey, Mrs. Darcy," Hope began as soon as Darcy was seated. "Mr. Steve and I are playing chutes and ladders and I'm winning," she chattered on as Darcy gazed at her, doing everything she could not to let Hope see her despair.

"Hope, go play in your room for a little while and then we'll finish our game," Steve said softly to the little girl as he placed a hand on her shoulder, gently turning her in the direction of her room. She scattered and left the adults alone in the living room. Steve angled his head, and his brows furrowed as he looked at Darcy. "Are you okay?"

"I had an appointment with the doctor this morning. He said he wants me on complete bed rest," she began as she stared blankly across the room.

"Is the baby all right?" Steve asked.

"Yes, the baby's fine." she answered, not volunteering any further information.

"Darcy, I don't understand why you seem so upset. If the baby's all right and you just need bed rest, what's troubling you?"

Shock from the doctor's orders gave way to anger at Steve's lack of understanding. She glared at Steve and snapped, "Bed rest means I must remain in bed. If I must remain in bed, then I won't be able to take care of this house and of Hope."

"Darcy, calm down," Steve said as he placed a hand on her shoulder. "I'll take care of you and Hope."

She inhaled sharply, rose from the sofa, and stomped to her room, slamming the door once she was safely behind it.

Darcy lay across the floral-print quilt on top of her bed. *Lord, what am I going to do? How am I going to get through this? Why have you allowed this to happen?* she thought as tears streamed down her cheeks. *How dare Steve say he'll take care of me? My husband promised to take care of me, and where is he? Why hasn't he called?* Question after question flew through her mind before exhaustion overcame her and she drifted into a fitful sleep.

*****

Hope emerged from her room when she heard the bedroom door slam. Her face etched with concern, she walked toward Steve, who sat on the living room floor oblivious to the approaching little girl. "Mr. Steve, where's Mrs. Darcy?" she asked as she plopped onto his lap. When he didn't respond, she reached up and, with her tiny hand, gently pulled his chin toward her. "Is Mrs. Darcy all right?"

Seeing the concern in her face, Steve smiled and pulled her close. "Yes, she's just tired." Steve looked around the room, trying to get his bearings. "Why don't we finish our game?" he asked, hoping the distraction would give him time to figure out what to do next.

*****

## Charleston, South Carolina

The tattered thin dark-blue blanket did little to warm the shiver traveling down Cindy's back as she sat on the cold steel bench staring at the metal bars before her. The taunts and jeers of the other inmates were just a buzz to Cindy. She was lost in thought and prayer. Her granny's words echoed through her mind, *You'll never be fulfilled in life by pursuing the love of a man. Only the love of God will fulfill your life. Stop chasing boys, and pursue God.* Somewhere deep in her heart, she knew her granny was right. *Lord, please forgive me for my foolishness. Open my eyes and heart, Lord. I want You. I need You.* She continued to silently pray until she heard her name mentioned and then her senses came to full attention.

"She's in the last cell on the right." *Clomp, clomp, clomp*, she heard as steps approached her cell, and *thump, thump, thump* she felt in her throat as her heart pounded in her chest. *What's going to happen now? Will I be going home?* Her thoughts were interrupted by the deep voice of the guard standing before the door of her cell.

"Mrs. Hogan, please come with me."

Cindy rose from the bench, the blue blanket falling to the ground. "Am I going home?"

The man acknowledged her question with a shake of his head. He opened the door and waited for her to arrive beside him. All too familiar with the procedure, Cindy stood beside the man, turned away from him, and placed her hands behind her back. The cold metal bracelets were soon secure, and the two began their journey down the hall, walking past jeers and crude comments from the other inmates. Without a word, Cindy was led outside the police department to a waiting unmarked car. The officer opened the back door and assisted her into the seat. She watched as he walked in front of the car and entered the driver's side. A moment later, the hum of the engine was the only sound to be heard. The officer never spoke a word as he pulled onto the highway. Cindy sat back as much as she could and tried to relax as she watched the scenery zip by the window.

Cindy's heartbeat rose as the car pulled into the parking lot of the Medical University of South Carolina. Her breathing grew labored and the color drained from her face. "Why are we here?" she managed, hoping her voice didn't reveal the fear rising within her.

The officer pulled the car into a parking space reserved near the front of the hospital, placed the vehicle in park, and opened the driver's door without a word. He walked around the front of the car and opened Cindy's door. "Mrs. Hogan," he began. "We've made arrangements for you to reside at a safe place until the trial is over, but you need to be checked out medically to make sure your injuries are healing. Once we leave the hospital, I'll take you to the safe house."

Confused, Cindy tilted her head and looked the officer in the eyes. "If I'm being taken to a safe house, why am I handcuffed?"

A slight smile crept across his face as his eyes softened. "We had to make it appear you were just being moved so your husband wouldn't know you're being released."

She nodded and stood in front of the officer, facing the car so he could remove the cuffs. Without a word, she followed him into the medical center.

*****

Steve and Hope were in the kitchen concocting something resembling dinner when their activities were interrupted by the ringing of the doorbell. Not expecting company, Steve looked to Hope and shrugged his shoulders. They wiped their hands on the dishtowel and proceeded toward the living room. Steve opened the door and was stunned to see Officer Riddle on the front porch. "Please, come in," Steve said as he stepped aside to allow him to enter. Officer Riddle stepped in and removed his hat. Immediately, his eyes landed on Hope who stood behind Steve.

"Hello, Hope. Do you remember me from the police department?" he asked, hoping to put the wide-eyed girl at ease. She only nodded her head.

"Hope, why don't you go back to the kitchen and place the slices of ham onto the tray," Steve said. Hope obediently skipped to the kitchen without question.

"Is everything all right?" Steve asked, wondering why the officer didn't just call.

"I have some information and need to talk to Darcy. Is she around?"

"She's lying down. The doctor has her on bed rest," he said as he led the officer to the bedroom. Steve quietly tapped on the door, cracked it open, and peered in before opening the door enough for the officer to see. "Darcy, Officer Riddle's here to talk to you. Are you up to visitors?"

Darcy nodded and Steve allowed the officer to enter the bedroom. Steve slipped from the room to give them privacy. Once Steve closed the door, Officer Riddle sat in the chair beside the bed. "Darcy, the Oakley Police Department's found your husband."

Darcy sat straight up in the bed. "Is he okay? When can I go to him?"

"Darcy, relax. We can't do anything today but pray."

"What about Cindy and her husband? Have they been found?"

"Yes, Mr. Hogan is behind bars at the Charleston Law Enforcement Center where he'll stay until his trial. Cindy will be placed in a safe house until the trial for her protection," he explained as he watched the concerned look on her face change to anger.

"Why isn't she being charged!"

The bedroom door opened just as she yelled and before the officer could explain. Steve entered the room with a tray of food for her. He placed it on the table beside the bed.

Officer Riddle ignored Steve. "Darcy, Cindy was kidnapped and beaten too. She's a victim just as much as Dillon. She's going to testify so we can prosecute Michael. She's the only one who can tell us exactly what happened."

"Is Cindy okay? What do you mean the only one, what about Dr. Collins?" Steve asked.

"Cindy's fine, just a little bruised and shaken. She's been seen at MUSC, and they're taking her to a safe house until after the trial. Dr. Collins is in a coma at the Magic Valley Regional Medical Center. He's in critical condition."

Darcy rose from the bed. "I have to go. I must go now. I have to be with my husband," she said as she frantically searched for a bag to throw some clothes in.

Steve grabbed her by the waist and guided her to the bed. "Darcy, you can't go right now. You need to think about your baby before you just take off. Let's call your doctor and see what he has to say."

Darcy realized he was right. She sat on the bed and turned to face Officer Riddle. Tears of relief flowed from her eyes that her husband was still alive. *Thank you, God, for returning my husband to me. Please, let him be okay.* "What happens now?" she asked, eager to be with him.

"Mr. Hogan will remain behind bars until his trial. The courts will be in touch with you every step of the way. Do you have any other questions?" he asked.

Darcy shook her head. "I'll call my doctor tomorrow and see if I'm able to travel. If he okays the trip, I'll head out there as soon as I can. I'll let you know when I can go."

"Hope and I will be traveling with her. I'm not going to let her go alone. I'll keep you informed of our plans," Steve said while never taking his eyes off Darcy.

Officer Riddle shook their hands and showed himself to the door. Once they were alone, Steve sat gently beside Darcy. "I'll contact the airlines and make arrangements once you hear from your doctor. I promise you we'll go as soon as we can, and you'll be sitting beside your husband before long," he reassured her, and she softly smiled and slowly lay back on the pillows.

*****

## Oakley, Idaho

"How's our patient?" the doctor asked as he scanned the chart at the end of the bed.

"He's about the same, no movement or signs of improvement," the nurse answered as she continued taking the patient's vital signs.

The doctor walked to the side of the bed as he read the chart. "Last night the police came by and said that they think he's the missing doctor from South Carolina. I think the officer said the Charleston Police Department is contacting the missing man's wife, and she's going to make arrangements to come here and positively identify he's her husband."

"That's good," she said as she finished his blood pressure.

"I hope they're correct and he's the missing doctor. I'd hate to see him suffer and possibly die alone," he said as he returned the chart to the foot of the bed.

The nurse didn't respond to the doctor's last comment. She continued her work, and the doctor soon left the room.

*Thank you, God. They finally know who I am. Please be with Darcy as she finds out what happened. Please cover her with Your comfort and grace. If it's Your will, Lord, find a way for her to be here with me. It would really be wonderful to hear her voice again.* Dillon prayed as the room fell silent once again. Within moments, he returned to his world of fitful sleep and dreams.

# CHAPTER 23

*Charleston, South Carolina*
*Two days later*

Startled by the sudden opening of the door, Darcy turned and was greeted by the smile of her doctor. "I didn't expect to see you for at least two weeks. I thought you'd be in bed, according to my orders, taking care of you and your little one," he said as he sat on the stool in front of the table.

"I've been resting," she said as she instinctively placed her hand on her abdomen and smiled faintly. "Steve's been great about taking care of Hope and all the household things."

The doctor nodded. "All right, if you're resting and you and the baby seem to be okay, what brings you to my office today?"

The sadness in Darcy's eyes spoke volumes. "I don't want to put the baby in danger, but I must go to Idaho immediately. The police have located my husband, and all I know is he's in a hospital in Idaho in a coma," she continued, her voice increasing with excitement.

The doctor placed his hand over Darcy's. "Darcy, we've been friends for a long time. Dillon's one of my dearest friends. I can't tell you if it's all right to go or not. I can tell you your condition will make it dangerous for you and the baby if you go. I can also tell you I know how much you love Dillon and how much he loves you."

Darcy sat, shivering from the coolness in the room or from anxiousness, she wasn't sure. She only knew she had to be with her husband, no matter the cost.

"You are only twelve weeks along and could easily lose the baby due to your blood pressure," he continued as he watched his friend's eyes brimming with tears, her arms wrapped around her shoulders, shaking. "I also know you'll worry yourself sick if you stay here. I'm sorry I can't be of more help, but it's going to be stressful for you and the baby either decision you make."

In all of Darcy's life, she had never had a truer friend than Edward. Edward and Dillon were best friends through college and medical school. Edward had been the best man at their wedding. Her thoughts drifted to their wedding. The white flowing gown, many shades of pink in her bouquet, the black tux Dillon wore with a matching hunter-green bow tie and cummerbund. Oh, how handsome he was, his eyes shining with love.

"Darcy, did you hear me?" Dr. Lattimore asked.

She gave her head a shake and returned her attention to the doctor. "I'm sorry, Ed, I was thinking of something else."

"I said I'd be praying for you all. If you travel slowly and promise to get plenty of rest, you'll probably be all right. However, if you feel the least bit different, tired, or develop a bad headache, go to the nearest emergency room, tell them of your situation, and have them call me immediately."

"Oh, thank you so much, Ed! I promise, if I feel anything strange, I'll seek immediate medical attention," she said as they hugged, and he left the room for his next appointment. Darcy felt a warm pleasure flood through her. She told herself she was considering the baby's well-being, and all would be well. She told herself Steve would travel with her and everything would be okay, but she knew deep inside, she only cared about being with her husband. Nothing and no one else mattered, not even the baby.

\*\*\*\*\*

"Hey Granny, how are you tonight?" Steve asked as she answered the phone.

"Stevie, it's good to hear from you. I've been thinking about you and Cindy all day. I was hoping you'd call." Unable to contain her excitement, she continued before Steve could say anything. "I prayed last night about a situation I need to talk to you about and prayed that if it was God's will, you'd call. Praise God! Will you be coming home soon?"

"It'll have to wait for a while. I called to tell you the police have found Cindy."

She gasped. "Is she all right? Where is she?"

"I think she's okay, Granny. The police have her in protective custody here in Charleston until her husband's trial. She's agreed to testify against him, so they're not charging her with a crime. A couple of officers from Charleston are flying to Idaho to investigate and gather information concerning the missing doctor. There may be charges in Idaho, but the kidnapping and assault charges here must be settled first."

"I'm so glad she's okay. I've been so worried about her. How is the doctor?"

"They think they've found him in Idaho. Darcy, Hope, and I are flying there to see if the man they found near Snake Canyon is Darcy's husband. We leave in the morning."

"Stevie, you need to be careful. You know how I feel about you staying with a married woman and now to have you traveling with her, what'll people think? It's not right."

Steve closed his eyes and slowly exhaled before explaining, "Granny, it's not like that. Darcy's allowing me to stay with her until we settle this matter. She needs help with Hope, the house, and herself, especially since she's pregnant. She's flying out with me because the police think they've found her husband at a hospital in Idaho. This man's in a coma and needs her if he's her husband. Hope's flying with us because we're all she has."

She didn't comment, apparently not satisfied with his answer. "Anyway, when you return, I have some particularly important things

I need to sit down and discuss with you and Cindy. Can you come home when you return?" she asked.

"I'll call you when we get back and plan a day when I can come home."

"Okay, tell Cindy I love her," she said.

"I don't know where she's is. She's at a safe house somewhere in Charleston, and I won't be able to see her. At least not right now."

"Okay, well, I'll be praying for both of you," she said and continued after a brief pause. "Stevie, be careful."

"Granny, planes are very safe today. You don't need to worry," he said, trying to reassure her.

"I'm not worried about your physical safety. It's your emotions I'm worried about. I love you and don't want to see you hurt. I only want the best for you."

"I know, Granny. I love you," he said and quickly hung up before she could respond.

*****

Steve prepared dinner and carried a tray to Darcy's room. She woke when she heard the squeak of the door. She smiled at him as she propped herself against the headboard and took the tray from Steve. "I really appreciate all you do around here. I don't know how I'd handle all this without your help."

"It's my pleasure. Hope is such an angel, and you need so little, I almost don't have enough to do," he said as he handed her the remote for the television and turned on the lamp on the nightstand. "I'm going to get Hope, and we're going to eat. Enjoy your dinner, and I'll check back with you in an hour or so and pack your bag for our trip in the morning." Her smile was thanks enough. He walked from the room and headed toward Hope's room.

Hope sat huddled on the full-size bed, leaning against the tan-colored wall, tears running down her small red cheeks. Footsteps echoed in the hallway and stopped at her door. She looked up just as Steve opened the door.

"What's wrong, honey?" he asked as he rushed to her side, wrapping her in his arms.

She shuddered in his hug. Steve held her, swaying back and forth, trying to soothe away her fears. "Hey, everything'll be okay. What's wrong?"

"I...I...I'm glad they found Mrs. Darcy's husband but...but... but...I don't want you to go away," she said between sobs.

"Oh, Hope, even when Dr. Collins comes home, I'll still be around. I'll always be here for you. I'll be like your uncle. I'm not going to leave you," he said as he rubbed her curly dark hair. *I'm worried about your emotions* echoed through his head as he recalled his granny's concern.

"I don't want you to be my uncle, I want you to be my daddy," she said as the sobs began again. At a loss for words, Steve held her until she was still. She had fallen asleep in his arms. He laid her on the pillow and covered her with the blanket at the foot of the bed. He rose and quietly left her room.

# CHAPTER 24

Steve led Darcy and Hope up the tiny aisle of the plane to their row. "Here we go, seventeen C, D, and E," he said as he motioned toward their seats. Darcy entered first and helped Hope into the middle. Steve placed the carry-on luggage in the overhead bin and settled next to Hope.

"I've never been on a plane before," Hope said as she wiggled and stretched her neck, looking up and down the aisles. "Is it like a big car? Will we go fast?"

Darcy and Steve exchanged a look of concern, realizing she didn't expect to leave the ground. "Soon, the doors will close, and you'll hear the big engines start. After the engines start, the plane will roll down this long road called a runway," Steve explained to the wide-eyed little girl. "We'll go faster and faster and then the pilot will guide the plane into the air. Once we're in the air you'll be able to see the clouds, and before you know it, we'll land in Idaho."

"Will we see heaven?" she asked as she turned her attention to Darcy.

Darcy reached toward her and stroked her cheek with her finger. "Heaven is way above the clouds. We can't see heaven until God calls us there."

"I can't wait to go to heaven. Will my mommy and daddy be waiting on me when I go to heaven?"

"Yes, they will. They'll be waiting with open arms for their little angel," Darcy said with a glow in her eyes that Steve never noticed before.

Moments later, the plane was in the air, and Hope was sound asleep. Steve glanced out the window at the blue sky passing by. When he turned back, he was met by Darcy's green eyes, watching his every move. "I just realized how little I know about you. You've been helping me for over two weeks, and I've been so focused on taking care of Hope and finding Dillon I haven't taken time to get to know you," she said as she smiled and glanced down at the child.

"There's not much to tell," he said. "I was born in Greenville, South Carolina, and I've been in the Navy since I graduated high school."

Her immediate instinct was to accept his answer and leave him alone, but she needed to know this man better—the man who had helped her with everything from the housework, cooking, and childcare to errands; the man who had shared her home the last two weeks. "I know you said your parents were killed. What happened?"

He took a deep breath. He had not thought about his parents for many years except for the moment in the police station. His chest tightened, and a lump filled his throat as memories of them filled his thoughts.

"I'm so sorry. I didn't mean to pry. I just wanted to get to know you better," she said but continued despite the awkwardness of the conversation. "What happened?"

He straightened slightly. Taking a deep breath, he aimed to slow his racing heart. "My parents were missionaries and were traveling home after a mission trip. Someone robbed and killed them in Sumter. They were found in the woods, all their belongings gone. They'd been stabbed multiple times. My grandmother always took care of us while they were away, so she just continued raising us," he said, being careful to keep his emotions deep inside, especially his anger toward God for allowing his parents to be killed while working for Him.

Darcy sucked in her breath. "Oh no, I'm so sorry."

Feeling a need to rescue her from this uncomfortable conversation, he continued. "Life is full of twist and turns. All we can do is make the best out of things. The only things we can be sure of are we're born and then die. Everything in between is just stuff."

She opened her mouth to ask him about his salvation when he abruptly stood. "Excuse me. I'll be right back," he said as he walked toward the back of the plane.

Darcy was asleep when he got back to his seat. Steve sat quietly, watching *The Way We Were* while Hope and Darcy slept. His thoughts continued to drift from the movie and returned to the words he heard earlier: *They'll be waiting with open arms. Did Darcy really believe in heaven and God? I wonder if there's something to this Jesus thing. He sure makes my granny happy. But look what believing in Him did for my parents. How could someone who's supposed to be love allow evil things to happen? It's just a fairy tale to help weak people make it through this world.* Confident this Jesus story was just that, a story, Steve laid his head back and drifted to sleep.

*****

Hope groaned, clutching her stomach and curling into a ball in her seat. Awakened by the commotion, Steve looked down at the little girl. She was obviously sick. Panic filled him as he looked around for someone to help. With everyone lost in their own world, he had no choice but to rouse Darcy. "Darcy," he said as he reached over and softly pushed on her shoulder.

"What?" Darcy said as she opened her eyes.

Steve didn't say a word. He looked down at Hope, and Darcy's eyes followed. She immediately knew what was wrong with her. Darcy rose from her seat, grabbed Hope's hand, and led her down the aisle as Steve stood and assisted her past his seat. Moments later, Steve could hear the retching coming from the restroom. It was just as he feared. *Thank goodness Darcy was here. That's not a job I care to do.*

A few moments later, the ladies returned. Steve stood to allow them access to their seats. "How are you feeling?" he asked the pale little girl standing before him.

"I'm better now," Hope told him, her voice high with excitement. "It was gross. You should have...," she stopped in midsentence when Steve put his hands over his ears and began shaking his head. Hope began to giggle. "Does that make you sick, Mr. Steve?" Knowing she had him, Steve shook his head yes and helped her into her seat.

Watching the whole scene, Darcy smiled and said, "You better get used to this kind of thing if you ever plan on marrying and having children."

"I wouldn't mind being married, but I don't think I'm daddy material," he said.

"You never know what God has planned for you," she said as she clasped Hope's buckle.

Not wishing to discuss God further, Steve glued his eyes to the screen as the last few minutes of the movie continued to play.

# CHAPTER 25

*Oakley, Idaho*

The following morning, Steve woke in the unfamiliar room. He glanced around taking in the blue curtains, a chest with a television on top, and the bed where Hope was curled up next to Darcy. Satisfied that the two were still asleep, he leaned his head back and closed his eyes.

It was late when the plane landed yesterday, and Steve had insisted they check into the hotel before venturing anywhere. Darcy had been disappointed, wanting to go straight to the hospital, but Steve's firmness won out; and they went to the nearest hotel for the night.

Steve heard a yawn and opened his eyes again, turning to check on the two ladies. His gaze met Darcy's and he smiled. "Are you still angry with me?" he asked.

Crossing her arms over her chest, she turned her head to look forward. "I should be," she answered. Then she turned her head back toward him and grinned. "But I'm not. You were right. I really needed the rest."

For just a moment, he felt warm inside, almost content. It was an odd, unexpected sensation. *Why do I care about this woman? I'm just taking care of her until her husband returns. Remember her husband? What's wrong with me?* He gave his head a quick shake, and

117

the feeling fled. "I'll go get breakfast while you shower and get ready. After breakfast, we'll go to the police department so the officer can accompany us to the hospital."

"Okay. I'll wake Hope, and we'll get ready," she said.

Steve rose already fully dressed and headed toward the door. "Steve?" Darcy called before he left. He turned and looked at her, waiting for her question. "I really appreciate everything you're doing to help me. I don't know what I'd do without you right now," she said, a blush rising to her cheeks.

He met Darcy's gaze and suspected she knew what he had been thinking just moments ago. He didn't like the way that made him feel, so he nodded his head and left as fast as he could. He didn't want or need more complications in his life. There was enough straighten out and deal with concerning his granny and sister. The last thing he needed was to fall for a pregnant married woman and the little girl she was raising.

*****

"Hi, I'm Steve Parnell, and this is Darcy Collins. We're here to see if the man hospitalized is Dr. Dillon Collins. We were told to come here so an officer can take us to the hospital to identify the gentleman," Steve said to the receptionist behind the glass partition at the police department in Idaho.

"Please have a seat, and I'll contact the chief for you."

Darcy walked toward the metal chairs lined against the cement wall and tried to get as comfortable as possible. Once she was seated, she lifted Hope onto her lap. Steve sat in the chair to Darcy's right.

Hope's eyes were wide as she reached and gently laid her hand on top of Steve's. He looked at the little dark-haired girl sitting beside him, her soft, warm hand on top of his. He peered into her eyes and smiled. Hope smiled back and climbed from Darcy's lap into Steve's lap. He held her close as Hope laid her head on his shoulder. Darcy's heart melted as she watched the interaction. *He's going to make a great dad one day.*

Darcy moved from the metal chair and paced the worn tiled floor, stepping to the door that led to a secluded long hallway. Sunshine tried to enter through the windows lining the block wall but was unsuccessful because of all the years of dirt blocking its way. She took a deep breath, trying to still her racing heart and shaking hands. *I should be in Charleston with Dillon, decorating the nursery for our bundle of joy. This just isn't fair!* She smoothed her hand up the nape of her neck as she continued to pace. *I must remain strong for our baby and Dillon.* She returned to her chair and picked up an old magazine and began to flip through the pages. After finishing the magazine, she began pacing again when an officer entered the room.

*****

Chief Teague entered his office and closed the door behind him. He sat in the red leather chair behind his desk and massaged his throbbing temples while taking a few deep breaths before his next task. *Some days I wonder why I ever chose to be an officer.* The hum of conversation from the hall filtered through his door, bringing him back to the present. *Sitting here isn't going to accomplish anything,* he thought as he rose and headed down the hall toward the people waiting for him in the reception room. The walk was a short one. He watched the lady pacing the floor and the man rocking a small child in his arms as he approached the room.

"Hi, I'm Chief Teague," he said as he shook the hand of the lady waiting for him at the doorway.

She took his hand. "I'm Mrs. Collins. This is Steve Parnell and Hope." She gestured to the little girl still snuggled against Steve's shoulder.

"Follow me to my office where we can talk privately," he said as he led them down the hall.

Nothing in all her born days had prepared Darcy for the pain and hurt of searching for her missing husband. She had prayed and prayed and finally felt her prayers were soon to be answered. Today she'd finally be able to see her beloved Dillon. *Lord, please help me through this difficult time so I can be with Dillon. Please bless him and comfort him no matter where he is. Lord, let him know I'm coming,* Darcy prayed as she, Steve, Hope, and Chief Teague entered the office and settled into the chairs.

"Mrs. Collins, I know you're anxious to see your husband," he said as he picked up the folder in front of him. "I'll have one of our officers take you to the hospital where he is in a few moments."

Trembling, Darcy looked at Steve. Her eyes were a portal to her thoughts and questions; he swallowed and eased his hand over hers. "Darcy, I won't leave you. I'll be with you until you bring your husband home."

Her breathing grew labored. The blood drained from her face, leaving her dizzy, but she refused to succumb to the faint feeling overwhelming her. "Thank you, Steve."

Chief Teague said nothing. He looked from Steve to Darcy, seeming at a loss for words. "When you're ready, Mrs. Collins, I'll escort you and Steve to the hospital, if it'll make you more comfortable," he said and continued before either could respond. "I think it best if you left Hope here with our social worker, Sandra. She's excellent with children."

"No, no!" Hope cried as she grabbed Steve's arm. "I don't want you to leave me. Please don't leave me."

"Honey, we won't leave you. You can go with us," he assured her as he picked her up and held her in his arms.

Darcy stood. Her legs wobbled, and Steve set Hope in the chair and had his arm around Darcy's waist to steady her before she collapsed.

"Are you all right, Mrs. Collins?"

"I think she needs to eat and rest a little while before we go to the hospital," Steve said, directing his comments to Chief Teague, not giving Darcy a chance to say anything. "She's expecting a child and is in a very fragile state right now," he continued holding her around the waist. "Darcy, let's go eat and let you lay down for an hour or so. Then we can come back and go see Dillon," he said as he led her toward the door.

Darcy wanted to jerk away from Steve and run to the hospital herself but was too weak to move. She didn't care that she needed to eat or rest. She didn't care about her needs or her baby's needs. She just wanted to be with her husband. All she could do was let Steve make the decisions for her right now, but as soon as she had strength, she was going to the hospital to be with her husband, regardless of how anyone else felt about it. She followed Steve and Hope from the room and sucked in a deep breath, then let it all out. There was more in life that was confusing than made sense right now, but all would be well when she returned to her life with her husband, Hope, and their little one on the way.

*****

Watching Steve wash Hope's hands and face after lunch reminded her of Dillon. Steve was gentle and loving in his actions, just as Dillon was. *Dillon will be a great dad. Thank you, Lord, for helping us find him. Please take care of him and help us get home safely.*

"Are you ready?" Steve asked Darcy as she stood, leaning in the doorway of the kitchen at the boarding house. She nodded, and the three of them headed to the rental car waiting for them in the driveway.

# CHAPTER 26

Try as she might, she couldn't keep the tears from spilling down her face. Steve reached for the tissues on the table beside the sofa and handed one to her. She nodded her appreciation as they continued to wait for the doctor. The door opened, and an elderly man wearing a long white coat entered the room.

"Hello, I'm Dr. Phillips," he said, making his way toward Darcy who stood to greet him. "I've been treating the man the police think may be your husband."

"Dr. Phillips, how is he?" she asked as Steve rose and stood beside her. "When can I see him?"

"Mrs. Collins, I know you're anxious to see if this is your husband, but we really need to talk before I take you to him," he said as he motioned for them to sit on the couch. Once everyone was seated, he continued. "This man's in very serious condition. He's hooked up to lots of tubes and machines. It's a really scary sight and may be upsetting for the little girl."

Darcy again rose from the sofa. "I just want to see him, please," she said as she grabbed the doctor's arm. "Please, take me to see him." Without another word, the four of them walked from the room and down the white, sterile hallway.

Moments later, they approached a room. Dr. Phillips stopped as he placed his hand on the doorknob. "Mrs. Collins, if this is your husband, please feel free to talk to him. Even though he's still in a coma, we believe he can hear. It may help," he said as he opened the door.

Mortification seeped into her being. She stood frozen at the door. The horribly distorted, bruised body lying before her couldn't be her husband. She stepped into the room and rounded the bed. Darcy made no pretense about being shocked. All color drained from her face as she took the seat close to the bed.

Unsure of who lay in the bed, Darcy reached out and touched the man's hand as she silently prayed for a sign. Moments passed, and she noticed the tattoo she had forgotten he had on his left bicep of a heart that contained their initials and wedding date. Tears streamed as shock and relief flooded her body upon the confirmation that this was her precious husband. "My sweet, sweet Dillon, I'm here," she said as she wiped a wisp of black hair from his forehead. "I'm here, darling and I'm not going to leave you."

Steve glanced at the man in the bed and was horrified at the sight of the person lying there. Before Hope could see into the room, Steve picked her up and carried her down the hall.

Dr. Phillips remained at the door as he watched Darcy sit in the chair beside the bed. "I'm going to check on a few other patients, Mrs. Collins. When I come back, we need to talk about a surgery your husband needs."

Darcy lifted her chin and glanced toward the doctor. She moistened her lips and opened her mouth but couldn't speak. Instead, Darcy closed her eyes and nodded once as she swallowed the tears threatening to spill down her cheeks.

Dr. Phillips turned and left the room.

Steve saw Darcy from the doorway as he returned after dropping Hope off at the nurse's station. He saw Darcy tenderly caress Dillon's face and heard her comfort the battered man with her words. He waited a few minutes before he entered the room.

Darcy glanced up as he came closer. "His hair's such a mess," she said as she pushed the dark locks away from his face. Try as she might, she couldn't stop the tears from flowing.

Steve sat in the chair on the opposite side of the bed. He shook his head as he surveyed the damage inflicted on this man by his sister's husband. *How could another human do something like this to a person?* "Darcy?" he said. She hesitated and then looked up at him. "Is there anything I can get you?"

Her expression revealed no emotion, and it seemed she had run out of tears. She paused only a moment before she returned to gently stroking her husband's face. "I have everything I need now that I'm with Dillon. I know he's in bad shape. He's a strong man and will fight this, especially once he learns he's going to be a daddy."

Darcy stared at Steve. Her stomach growled, and she glanced at the clock across the room.

"Darcy, I'm going to go to the cafeteria and get you some food. While I'm gone, I'll call Officer Riddle and let him know this man is your husband and tell him how he can get in touch with us if he needs anything for his investigation," Steve said as he rose from the chair and started toward the door.

"Wait," she said, and he paused by the foot of the bed and turned to face her once again. The stress of the situation etched in her face tore at his heart. He inhaled deeply, struggling to keep the urge to go to her side and comfort her pushed deep inside him. *The last thing she needs is someone else to worry about, but how I wish I could take some of this stress and worry off of her.* "Would you mind doing me a favor since you're calling Charleston anyway?" she asked.

"No, I don't mind. What is it?"

"Will you call my pastor for me and ask him to start a prayer chain for Dillon and update him on the situation for me? I really don't want to leave him now that I'm here with him," she asked as she looked at Steve, but her hand never stopped smoothing Dillon's hair.

"Yes, of course I will," he said and left the room before she could respond and before she could see the tears forming in his eyes.

*****

"Mrs. Collins, are you ready to talk?" Dr. Phillips asked as he entered the room and began writing notes on his chart.

Darcy's shoulders rose and fell like bellows fanning a flame. "I want my husband to have the best of care. Do whatever you have to in order to make him better."

He gave a slow nod. "Mrs. Collins, I'll do everything in my power, but you have to understand, your husband is very sick. He may not make it through the surgery." The room was silent except for the constant beep of the heart monitor. The weight of the doctor's words pressed on her like a ton of bricks. *My husband could die. Oh, dear Lord, no. Please don't take him. I just found him. We have our entire life ahead of us. You can't do this to me.*

"Mrs. Collins, did you hear me?" the doctor asked, bringing her from her private thoughts.

"No, I'm sorry. What did you say?"

"Mr. Collins needs surgery on his right leg. The injuries are severe. I'm not sure if the surgery will repair the injuries. We may have to amputate."

"No! No, I don't want you to amputate his leg. He's supposed to get better now since I'm here. I don't want him to have surgery or lose his leg!" she yelled just as Steve entered the room with her food.

"Darcy, what's wrong?" Steve asked as he placed her food on the table at the foot of the bed.

Steve stepped over to Darcy. "They may have to take his leg," she said as she hugged her knees to her chest like a frightened small child.

"I know you're scared," he said as he placed his hands on her shoulders to comfort her. "Is the surgery really necessary now?" he asked the doctor who stood quietly on the other side of the bed.

"Without the surgery, we can't correct the damage done to his leg, and infection has already set in. We are having a difficult time fighting it. If we don't do the surgery soon and at least stabilize the leg and clean out the infection, he'll die," the doctor said as compassionately as he could.

"I know you don't want him to have surgery, but he needs it," Steve said as he kneeled beside her. The doctor and Steve waited several minutes while Darcy cried.

"Promise me you'll do all you can to save his leg," she said as she grabbed a tissue from the table beside her and wiped her eyes.

"Mrs. Collins, I promise to do everything in my power to take care of your husband," the doctor said as he returned the chart to the peg on the foot of the bed. "I'll get the nurse to bring in the consent forms, and we'll begin as soon as possible."

"Thank you," Steve said as the doctor left the room. "Darcy, I'm going to step out so you can have some private time with your husband before the surgery. I'll also go and call the pastor again for you and let him know about the surgery and check on Hope," Steve said as he stood to leave.

"Where is Hope?" she asked, realizing she hadn't seen her in quite a while.

"She's fine. She's made friends with the nurses, and they're watching after her until we leave."

Darcy nodded and was left alone—alone with the man she loved, alone with her memories, alone.

*****

Darcy rose from the chair beside the bed and walked to the sink. She found a cloth and wet it with cold water. After wringing the cloth, she returned to her husband's bedside. "It seems like a life-time ago when we were lying in bed talking about all the children we wished for. That was our first argument, do you remember? I wanted three and you wanted five. After a few moments of my pouting, you proposed a compromise, and we settled on four. We talked like we were in control of everything. We were so full of hopes and dreams. If someone had told me then we'd be where we are today, I'd have told them they were crazy," she said in a whisper as she wiped his bruised face.

Just then, the door opened, and two men in green scrubs walked in, pushing a gurney. "They're waiting for him in the operating room," the taller of the two men said as they began the task of transferring the unconscious man onto the gurney.

"Wait," Darcy said as they headed toward the door. "Can I have just one more moment with him?"

"Make it quick. They're waiting for him."

Without hesitation, Darcy stepped to the side of the gurney. The men in the green scrubs stepped aside. "Dillon, sweetheart, I love you and will be praying while you're in surgery." She tucked a strand of hair behind her ear. "Honey, stay strong. We need you. Did you hear me? We need you. Dillon, fight this with all you have because you're not fighting for just me. You're fighting for our baby," she said as she squeezed his hand three times.

"We really need to go, ma'am."

Darcy leaned forward and kissed her husband on the forehead. A single tear escaped his eye and rolled down his cheek. *Did he hear me? Does he know about the baby?* She stood and wondered as she wiped the tear away. The men returned to the gurney and started pushing it out the door. She watched as the men rushed him from the room and away from her once again.

\*\*\*\*\*

*Baby? Is my Darcy pregnant? Lord, please help me. I want to be here for my baby and Darcy,* Dillon thought as he was pushed through a set of double doors into a cold room. *Ouch!* he yelled for only his ears as a burning sensation crept up his arm, and he drifted into darkness.

\*\*\*\*\*

The chief strode down the hall, looking in each room for the visiting officer. "Where's the officer from Charleston?" he asked the officer sitting at the front desk. The officer at the desk pointed to a room two doors further down the hall. Chief Teague headed toward the room with the files in his hands.

"Would you like some coffee?" the chief offered as he entered the room.

"Sure, thanks," Officer Riddle said as he sat in the white plastic chair attached to the long-speckled table. The chief grabbed two cups from the cabinet and filled them. "Well, I'm Chief Teague," he said as he offered him one of the coffees.

"Thank you," he said as he took the hot cup from the man. "I'm Officer Riddle from Charleston."

After Chief Teague sat down across from the other officer and they both had a few moments to drink the stout dark drink Chief Teague called coffee, Officer Riddle broke the silence. "What a horrible situation this is."

Chief Teague nodded his head in agreement. After a few more sips of the hot liquid, he opened one of the files and turned it toward Officer Riddle. "Here are the reports, copies of the warrants, statements from Cindy Hogan and Michael Hogan's brother Alex, and other evidence and information we have collected regarding this case."

Officer Riddle slid the folder closer, scanning the information. "I really appreciate all of the work you guys have put into this case. Can you tell me more about Mr. Hogan's brother Alex?"

Chief Teague nodded and began telling him everything he could remember and offered to take him to Alex's home so more information could be gathered.

"Once I talk with Alex, I'll head back to Charleston and add this new information to our files for the case we are building against Mr. Hogan."

The officers finished their coffee, discarded the trash, and left to go see Alex.

*****

"Lord God, please protect my husband. Give him strength to endure this surgery. Oh Lord, please be with the surgeons, giving them wisdom to save him. I commit our lives, our hopes, our dreams, and our future to you," Darcy prayed, her eyes open, staring at the now vacant bed where her prince once lay. Willing herself to relax, she sensed someone watching her. Shifting her weight, she stared at the figure in the doorway.

"Did the doctor say how long the surgery would take?" Steve asked as he entered the room and sat on the foot of the bed, facing Darcy.

She sighed hard knowing she shouldn't allow the anger inside her to stay. She knew the Sovereign One was in control. She just couldn't understand why He would allow such a man of grace, honor, and faith be hurt like this. "I don't know. They said it would probably be hours."

Steve rose from the bed and took Darcy by the hand. "Come on, let's go to the cafeteria. You need to eat something to keep your strength up."

"No, I can't leave his room. The doctor might come back, and I want to be here the minute Dillon wakes."

"Darcy, they just took him down for surgery. Like you said, it could be hours before they bring him back. You need to eat, if not for you, for your baby," Steve said as he knelt on one knee so he could look her in the eyes. "Darcy, I'm not giving you a choice. Get up and let's go to the cafeteria and eat. If you don't, I'm going to carry you to the cafeteria."

His firmness and concern brought a faint smile to her lips. She knew he was right again. She wrapped her arms around her middle and rose from the chair. Steve led her from the room. They stopped by the nurse's station and gathered Hope so she could join them.

*****

A few minutes later, Steve, Hope, and Darcy arrived at the cafeteria. After making their way through the line, they headed toward a small table near the rear corner. Steve sat his tray on the table and pulled the chair out for Darcy. Without a word, she sat down and stared at her plate while Steve went for napkins. An uncontrollable shiver caught her off guard as reality began to sink in. *My husband's been returned to me. It won't be long, and we'll be home, home together,*

*together with our precious little one and Hope.* She sighed and pulled herself closer to the table just as Steve returned.

"Are you okay?" he asked as he sat in the chair across from Darcy.

Darcy looked around the room. "Sometimes, it seems like I'm going to wake up and all of this will have been a dream. It feels like I'm in the middle of a movie and none of this is really happening," she said as she turned to look at Steve while he helped place food in front of Hope.

"Darcy, tell me about Dillon," he said. "I know he's your husband and a doctor, but tell me about him. What's he like?"

Darcy couldn't help but smile as she thought of her wonderful husband. "Oh, Steve, you'd really like him. He's the most loving, caring, and forgiving man I've ever met. He always said blaming people had no purpose. That we should learn to deal with circumstances instead of wasting our time finding people to blame for our problems. He's a perfect example of God's grace. People would say or do things that made me angry, and he'd comfort me by saying God sent His son to die for me and my sins were forgiven by God's grace, and I should forgive others just as Christ forgives me." Her smile faded as her thoughts drifted.

Steve glanced down at his food. He picked up his fork and began picking at the morsels on the plate. "I'm so sorry you're going through all of this. I wish there was something I could do to help."

"Steve, you've been a big help to me. I don't know how I would've managed without you. God sent you just when I needed someone most."

Steve stared across the room as he slowly lifted his cup and sipped on the steaming coffee. "Darcy, do you really believe God is real?"

"Yes, Steve, I do. Without God's strength and mercy, I couldn't make it through all of this. I'm not as strong in my faith as Dillon, but I'm striving to grow closer to Him and learning to trust Him."

Steve opened his mouth to speak, but the chiming of a clock in the distance distracted Darcy from the conversation.

"I need to get back to Dillon's room. I don't want to miss the doctor when he finishes the surgery," she said as she rose and headed toward the elevator. Steve quickly cleared the table, grabbed Hope's hand, and followed her.

"Hold up," he yelled as he walked as quickly as he could with Hope in tow to catch up with Darcy.

\*\*\*\*\*

## Charleston, South Carolina

"Mrs. Hogan, here's another blanket," the lady said as she walked into the bedroom.

Cindy watched her enter the room and offer the blanket. She struggled to keep her voice calm while her insides screamed, *I want out of this place!* "Have you heard anything from my brother?" she asked, desperate to find out any information concerning him, the doctor, or her husband. Her mind drifted to memories of her husband and the good times they had together, even though they were very few. *I hope he's okay and not being mistreated. He really is a great guy. People just don't understand him like I do. If I hadn't made him mad, we wouldn't be in this situation.*

"The last I heard, your brother was at the hospital with the doctor's wife. I think they were taking the doctor in for surgery."

Cindy stared at the lady as her words echoed in her head. "What about my husband? Have you heard anything about how he's doing?"

"Cindy, you know you can't have any contact with your husband, and we're not allowed to give you information or help you correspond with him in any way. Don't you remember your deal with the district attorney?" the lady said as she sat on the bed beside her, gently touching her shoulder.

Cindy instinctively recoiled at the touch. She was so used to being pushed around and hit that even gentle touches still scared her. "If you hear from my brother or hear anything about Dr. Collins, will you let me know?"

The lady nodded her head as she stood to leave. As she reached the door, Cindy blurted out, "He's not a bad person. You don't know him like I do. He wouldn't intentionally hurt anyone. When he's not drinking, he's a really great person."

The lady closed her eyes and left the room.

*****

## Oakley, Idaho

"How are you holding up?" Steve asked as he and Darcy entered Dillon's room to wait for the doctor to update them concerning the surgery.

"I'm tired, but I feel a little better since getting something to eat," she said as she returned to the small chair beside her husband's hospital bed.

"Darcy?" Steve asked, his heart beating so loud he could hear it in his ears.

Darcy glanced up, her red eyes locked as she turned her attention to him. Moments passed, and silence filled the room.

Steve inhaled sharply, blinked his eyes as he searched for the courage to ask her the heavy question on his heart. "With everything happening, why do you still believe in God?" he asked, exhaling and allowing his shoulders to relax. *Well, now that can of worms is open.*

A slight smile creeped across Darcy's mouth as she tilted her head and continued to look at Steve. "I'm sorry, I just don't understand how a God who's supposed to love people could allow such horrible things to happen, especially to someone as kind and loving as you."

Darcy slowly nodded her head and looked around the room. Her eyes fixed on a painting hanging on the wall facing Dillon's bed. "See the picture there?" Steve's eyes darted to the object of her attention, and he nodded his head. "That picture wouldn't exist without a creator, right?" she asked.

"Yes," he hesitantly agreed. "But how does that prove God exists?"

"See, nothing would exist without a creator. I believe God created the universe, and no matter which theory you wish to trust, whether it's the big bang or creation, God had to create the materials for the world to exist," she said and continued before he could respond. "Not only do I believe He created the world, I also believe each of us are born with a God-shaped hole in our hearts that longs for love and acceptance. I believe God places the hole there so we'll search for Him, and when we find Him, He fills your life with peace and love like you've never felt before. No matter what's going on in the world, you know there's a higher power who loves you and will always be there for you."

Steve returned his gaze to Darcy. Quiet filled the room as he allowed her words to fill his thoughts. *I'll give her that, someone had to create this crazy world.*

"Are you okay?" she asked.

The sound of her voice brought Steve back to the present. "I'm sorry," he said as he straightened in the chair and ran his hand through his hair. "I guess I'm still struggling with how a loving god could allow so many bad things happen to those he loves."

Darcy slowly nodded her head. "Let me ask you a question. Why would God allow good things happen to bad people?"

Stunned by her question, Steve knit his brows together, narrowed his eyes, and looked at her. "I've never thought about it like that."

"First Corinthians 13:12 says, 'Now we see things imperfectly, like puzzling reflections in a mirror, but then we will see everything with perfect clarity. All that I know now is partial and incomplete, but then I will know everything completely.' See, we don't have to understand why God allows things to happen because the world is full of humans with free will. Sometimes people chose to do bad things which affects others," Darcy paused.

The only sound in the room was the ticking of the clock as Steve pondered what she said. "That makes sense, but how do you know for sure God loves you?" he asked as he interlaced his fingers behind his head and leaned his hand back, resting it in his hands.

"I believe in God because He has made me into something I could never be on my own, and I have seen people change once they trust in Him and allow Him to live in their hearts," she said as she covered her mouth with her hand to hide a yawn.

"I'm sorry," Steve said as he realized how tired she was. "I know you're tired and have more to worry about than my questions. Why don't you try to rest?"

"I am tired. Would you mind if we talked about this later?" she asked as she took the blanket from the chair beside her and placed it over her lap and laid her head to the side of the chair. A few moments later, she was asleep.

Steve stood and eased out of the room, careful not to wake her. *Pastor Watson, I hope you're not busy. I really need to talk with you.*

*****

Steve returned to the hospital room and tried to quietly open the door, but he couldn't stop the squeak of the hinge.

Darcy sat up straight with fear in her eyes. Steve looked at her, alarmed by the sudden movement. "Where's Hope?" Darcy asked.

Sighing with relief upon understanding her fear, he explained how the nurses graciously offered to watch Hope while Steve and Darcy were in Dillon's hospital room. Satisfied with his answer and tired from all the activity, she curled into the chair and quietly dozed.

Steve eased through the door so Darcy could sleep. He searched his pocket for the phone number to the safe house. He was walking toward the public phone to call them and ask about his sister when he saw the doctor walk into the room where Darcy lay sleeping. He quickly turned around and raced after the doctor.

*****

Darcy opened her eyes and tried to focus as the door to her husband's hospital room opened. She watched the doctor, the way he tried to shut the door behind him, but Steve entered before the door could be shut. Dr. Phillips turned and their eyes met. The expression on his face told her what he was struggling to say.

"Mrs. Collins, I'm so sorry. We did everything we could, but your husband wasn't strong enough and didn't make it through the surgery."

She stood; the words weighed on her like a ton of bricks. She could hardly catch her breath. The room began to spin as memories of Dillon came flooding through her mind. "No!" she screamed as she fell to her knees.

# CHAPTER 27

*Charleston, South Carolina*

Cindy spooned soup into her mouth from the ceramic bowl. *Where's my brother? Why hasn't he called? Lord, why are You not taking care of me?* Her thoughts were interrupted when the gentle lady who ran the place entered the kitchen. "Has anyone heard from my brother?" she asked as the lady sat in the chair at the table across from her.

"He just called," she said as she looked into Cindy's eyes. The quiet was deafening for a moment as the woman struggled to speak. "Cindy, I just hung up with your brother. Dr. Collins passed away this afternoon."

Cindy sat and stared at the lady. Many responses came to her mind but none she dared to voice out loud. *A gentle answer...* kept popping into her mind. "No, no. He can't be dead. I've been praying for him. God couldn't have let him die. It wasn't his fault. It was all my fault," she said. Her voice grew more and more panicked as she continued. "If I hadn't called him, he never would've been at my house. If I hadn't made Michael mad, I wouldn't have needed the doctor. Why did I call him?" she yelled and broke into uncontrollable sobs. She ran to her room, shutting the door behind her and collapsing onto the bed. *It's all my fault,* she repeated to herself as she sobbed until exhaustion overtook her and she drifted into sleep filled with visions of the doctor and his battered body.

*****

*Oakley, Idaho*

The shock was more than Darcy could handle. She felt as if she had fallen into some strange dreamworld. *Why would God allow me to find him and then take him from me?* Now Dillon was dead. There would be no more them, no more children. She felt her life ended with his.

Steve stood in the doorway and stared at Darcy, crumpled in a heap at the foot of the hospital bed, sobbing into her hands, yelling "Why, why, why?" Moving quietly, Steve settled beside her on the floor, unsure how to comfort her. "Darcy, I don't know why this has happened, but I'm here for you and will help you through this." Darcy glared at him, and anger blazed through her eyes.

"It happened because your sister called my husband to help her because she allowed her husband to beat up on her. If she were any type of a woman, she would never had allowed herself in such a situation. It's all her fault," she yelled and pulled away from him.

Stunned, Steve didn't move. Moments passed which felt like hours as Darcy curled into a ball and continued to cry. Steve slowly inched toward her and gently placed his hand on her shoulder. Touched by his kindness after lashing out at him, she raised her head and leaned into his chest and cried while he held her in his arms.

*****

"I'll be bringing Cindy home soon, Granny," he sighed and placed his glass on the table beside him. "Granny, please calm down. I know you're excited about us coming home. I do...I understand you have something important to tell me, but what you don't understand is Darcy's husband died during surgery yesterday. It's going to be a while before we'll be back in South Carolina. I know, Granny. I love you too. I will…I'll tell her as soon as we hang up. Bye." Steve returned the phone to the cradle. He walked in a daze to the bedroom where Darcy lay. The darkness hid the stress and fear on his face. "The coroner's office is going to release Dillon's body tomorrow. I'll make arrangements for us to fly back with his body," he said as he sat on the edge of the bed. "Darcy, is there anything I can get for you?"

Darcy rolled over, turning away from Steve. "Get away from me. If it wasn't for your sister and her husband, Dillon would still be alive," she yelled as her body convulsed into sobs. He pulled her toward him. Her resistance halted when she felt the strength from his arms.

"It'll be okay," he whispered as he held her head against his chest, ignoring the accusations against his sister.

*****

"Officer Riddle, it's Steve Parnell."

"Hey, Steve. I heard about Mrs. Collins's husband. How is she?"

"She's okay, considering the circumstances. She's asleep right now. I need a favor, and you're the only one I can think of who may be able to help."

"I'll do whatever I can."

"I haven't been able to speak with my sister. They'll only take messages and give them to her at the safe house. I'm really worried about her. Is there any way you can check on her and make sure she knows what's going on and see if she's okay?"

"Sure, I'll stop by there today and talk with her in person. Is there anything special you want me to relay?"

"Yes, please. Will you let her know I need to stay here and help Darcy with the arrangements to get her husband home. And if you don't mind, tell her I'm here for her and I love her."

"Yeah, I'll do that for you. Is there a number I can call you back if there's a problem?"

"No, I don't know how long we'll be at the hospital later, and when we leave there, I'll be trying to arrange for a flight home. I guess I'll just call you when I have a chance later tonight or when we get back to Charleston, if that's okay?"

"Yeah, sure. Just call whenever you can. I'll check on your sister. Tell Darcy I'll be praying for her."

"Thanks, I really appreciate your help," Steve said and hung up the phone. *Praying for her? What is it with these people and prayer? Do they really believe prayer works? It hasn't worked so far. Look where it's gotten Dillon.* Steve walked to the living room and sat on the couch. Hope was outside playing and Darcy sound asleep in her room. He sat in the quiet, lost in his thoughts. *I don't know much about You, God, but if You're real, please be with Darcy. Help her broken heart. Protect her and her baby.*

# CHAPTER 28

*Oakley, Idaho*

I t seemed her whole world was crashing down around her. Not long ago, she was cooking her husband's favorite meal for their anniversary and now she sat on the noisy large plane heading toward home. Sitting beside her was a stranger named Steve and a little girl who needed her and her husband's body's below. Below with the luggage. *Lord, help me!* Darcy screamed inside. *I miss him so much.* She leaned her head against the tiny window. The hum of the plane lulled her to sleep.

*****

*Charleston, South Carolina*

"No!" Cindy screamed and was startled awake as she gasped, inhaling deeply, exhaling slowly, trying to slow her racing heart. Visions of Dr. Collins's distorted body haunted her dreams.

Hearing her screams, the lady who ran the safe house entered Cindy's room. "Are you okay?" she asked, her voice filled with concern.

Rolling to her side, Cindy slowly pushed herself upright, still shaking from her dream. "I think so. It was just a horrible nightmare."

Satisfied her tenant was okay, the woman turned to leave the room, informing Cindy breakfast was ready if she was hungry.

"Thank you," Cindy said as the door closed. She sat on the bed, remembering her dream. She began searching her heart for the truth. She knew she was at fault for this as much as her husband. She was thankful the authorities had decided not to press charges against her in exchange for her testimony. The words from her granny, many years ago, haunted her thoughts. *Cindy, it's easy to blame others for our circumstances. It takes a mature person to accept their responsibility for their actions which lead to all situations.* Cindy pondered those words of wisdom. It finally clicked with her. *I chose to marry Michael. I know he's mean when he drinks. I've made excuses for him since the first day of our marriage. As of today, there'll be no more excuses. I'm going to do all I can, with God's help, to make things right with my brother and if possible, with Mrs. Collins. Today, I'll become the woman God has wanted me to be all along.*

"Cindy, breakfast is getting cold," the female voice floated through the air, interrupting her thoughts.

*****

Darcy allowed herself to be led from the plane and through the airport like a child. Once they were in the car on the way to Darcy's house, she looked at Steve and asked, "Steve, why are you doing this?"

Not sure what to say, Steve remained quiet for a moment as he drove the familiar roads toward her home. Finally, he answered, "Darcy, I don't know why we've come into each other's lives, but I promised you to help you through this, and I'm a man of my word." His tone very businesslike. "I can't imagine how difficult this is for you. I want to make sure you take care of yourself and the little one you're carrying. I also want to help take care of Hope."

Darcy looked at the tiny sleeping figure in the back seat. "You've done such a great job taking care of her. She's been so good and quiet, I almost forgot she was with us."

Unsure if he should reveal how he really felt, he fought between keeping silent or sharing his true feelings with her. Sharing his feelings won the battle. "It grieves me to feel so helpless to ease your pain. I know the next few days and months will be the most difficult for you, but I promise I'll be here to help you," he said without taking his eyes from the road.

She softly smiled. "Thank you," she said barely above a whisper.

"After you rest for a while, we'll sit down and make all the arrangements for Dillon's funeral," he said as he patted her hands, which were placed in her lap.

Silence filled the car for the remainder of the ride to Darcy's house. Steve parked in front of her home, got out, and went immediately to the passenger door. He opened it and offered his hand to help Darcy from the car. She accepted his hand and allowed him to lead her to the front door. After seeing her securely inside and comfortably seated on the couch, he left to get Hope, who was still sleeping in the back seat. Within moments, he had everyone in the home, as well as the luggage. "Why don't you lie down for a few moments while I unpack these bags, and then I'll bring you something to eat."

Without a word of protest, Darcy rose from the couch and walked to her room. She lay on her bed, pulled Dillon's pillow to her chest, and cried herself to sleep.

*****

"Hey Granny, it's Steve," he said as he collapsed onto the couch.

"Oh, Stevie. You sound so tired."

"I am, Granny. We finally made it back to Charleston. Darcy and Hope are sleeping, so I wanted to take a moment to call you."

"How's Cindy?"

"I don't know. I haven't been able to speak with her. I can only leave messages. However, Officer Riddle told me he would check on her, and I should be talking to him later today. I'll call you again later and let you know what he has to say."

"Okay, honey. Is there anything I can do?"

Chuckling, he said, "That's actually why I'm calling. Can you come to Charleston and help me for a little while?" he asked.

"Sure, honey. I can head out in the morning and should be there midafternoon."

"I'd really appreciate it," he said as he gave her directions to Darcy's house. "Once you get here, I'll introduce you to Officer Riddle, and he'll take you to see Cindy. See, she's at a safe house, but I can't see her because the safe house is also a battered women's shelter, and men aren't allowed to know where it's located. Officer Riddle said due to the circumstances, they'd allow you to visit with her."

"Of course, I will. I'd love to see both of you. You guys are my world. Will I be able to spend some time with you?"

"Yes, we'll get together. I'll introduce you to Darcy, and if you still want to talk about whatever it was you wanted to talk about a few days ago, we can do that also."

"Sure, honey. I'll pack now and get ready to hit the road first thing in the morning."

"Thanks, Granny. I'm glad I can always count on you."

"I love you, Stevie. I'll see you tomorrow."

"Okay. I love you too, Granny. Bye," he said as he hung up. He stood staring at the phone thinking how lucky he was to have someone in his life who loved him so much and so unconditionally. *What an amazing woman.*

*****

"Where are we going?" Michael barked as the officer cuffed his hands behind his back before unlocking the cell again.

"You have to appear before the judge," the officer answered, and he pushed the foul-smelling man toward the door.

"I ain't going before no judge. I haven't seen my attorney since my second night here."

"Your attorney will be waiting for you in court."

"Why are we going to court?" Michael asked as he tried to pull away from the officer.

The officer tightened his grip and kept walking toward the rear of the police department. Moments later, the two arrived in the parking lot, and the officer shoved Michael into the backseat of the police car, buckling him in before getting into the car himself. It was only a few blocks to the courthouse, and the officer was thankful for the short drive so he didn't have to suffer from the stench of the prisoner in the backseat for long. He pulled into the parking lot, exited the vehicle, and opened the back door.

"I already said I ain't going in front of a judge until I see my attorney," he yelled as spittle hit the officer's face.

Anger flashed through the officer's eyes as he wiped his face. He grabbed the prisoner by the forearm and shoved him forward. "You have no choice. Now move!" he yelled and led Michael into the building. They stopped in front of the two oak doors that led to the courtroom. A security guard saw them coming and opened the door for them. The officer nodded his thanks and continued his journey to the large desk before him.

Michael recognized his attorney and took the seat next to him. He wasn't able to sit for long. The judge entered the room. "All rise," the bailiff stated. Everyone except Michael immediately stood. Michael's attorney grabbed him by the arm and pulled him to his feet.

"Be seated," the judge said as he took his seat behind the large desk at the front of the room. "Mr. Hogan, you've been brought before me because the man you kidnapped and savagely beat has died, and you're being charged with murder."

"Murder!" Michael screamed as he jumped up from his chair.

"Sit down, Mr. Hogan," his attorney said, pulling him by the arm to pull him back to his seat.

"I ain't killed nobody, and you ain't got no proof I hurt or kidnapped anyone," he said as he returned to his seat.

"That'll be for the jury to decide. For your information, Mr. Collins died yesterday during surgery. His death is because of the injuries he sustained due to the beating he endured," the judge explained. Michael sat quietly, staring at the judge. "If there are no further questions, we'll be adjourned," the judge said as he banged his gavel and rose from the bench.

"Where's my wife? I want to see my wife," Michael said before the judge could finish.

"Mr. Hogan, you're restrained from having any contact with your wife at this time. If you have any questions, you can address them with your attorney." The judge turned toward his attorney, "Mr. Hogan needs to return to the LEC to be booked on the new charge."

"Yes, sir," the attorney said as he told his client to stand up.

The judge dismissed the hearing and left the courtroom.

"Why didn't you say something?" Michael barked at his attorney.

"Mr. Hogan, there's nothing we can say at this point. The best thing you can do is keep your cool. I'll visit you at the jail, and we'll start working on your defense," he said as the officer who brought Michael to the courtroom arrived at the attorney's side. The attorney stepped aside, allowing the officer to take the prisoner back to his cell.

# CHAPTER 29

The sound of the shutting car door caused Steve and Hope to stop in their tracks. They were both laughing and sweaty from their game of tag. They walked through the back gate into the front yard just in time to see the elderly woman exiting the car. "Granny!" Steve yelled with excitement as he walked toward the little old lady.

Hope stood by the gate and watched as the two hugged each other. Steve motioned for Hope to join them, and the spry little girl didn't hesitate. Soon she was standing beside Steve as he introduced her to his grandmother. The threesome walked into the house. Once inside, Steve sat with his granny in the living room, and Hope ran to her room to play. "Remember to play quietly so Mrs. Darcy can rest," he reminded her. Steve and his granny stayed in the living room and continued their small talk.

*****

"Thanks for making lunch, Granny. It was wonderful," Steve said as he pushed away from the table. "I've really missed your cooking."

"It was yummy, Mrs. Parnell," Hope said as she took the last bite of her biscuit and soaked it in the white gravy left on her plate. "I've never had this white soupy stuff."

146

"That's gravy, honey," Steve said as he chuckled at the little girl.

"Gravy," she said with a mouthful. Both Steve and his granny laughed at her enjoyment of such a simple meal.

"Granny, just relax. I'm going to take Darcy a plate and check on her. When I finish, I'll clean up the kitchen, and we'll call Officer Riddle and see about getting you to the safe house to visit with Cindy."

"That'll be wonderful," she said as she watched her grandson prepare a tray and leave the kitchen. Once alone, she rose from her chair and started clearing the dishes. By the time Steve returned to the kitchen, she had finished the task.

"Granny, I told you I'd do the dishes," he scolded.

"I know but I'm not helpless, and you have plenty to do. Besides, I'd like to see Cindy as soon as I can."

He smiled as he led her to the living room. Once they were settled, he picked up the phone and dialed the familiar number.

*****

She watched the passing scenery as the car drove down the two-lane road. The ocean slowly growing as they approached. The sunset caught her attention, and she got lost in thought as she watched the sun dip below the horizon. The glowing sun, a crisp circle in the bloody sky, illuminated a quivering path across the water. It bathed the ocean's meek waves and the wispy clouds in a burning red as the fleeting colors of dusk began to fade away. Memories of watching Steve and Cindy growing up and growing closer after the tragic death of their parents bounced through her mind. Within moments, the car slowed and parked in front of the beautiful brick building.

"Mrs. Parnell, we're here," Officer Riddle said, jarring her from her thoughts. He exited the car, assisted her out, and walked her to the front door. He rang the bell, and within seconds, the door opened, and they were welcomed into the home. The door closed and locked behind them.

What followed was a joyful chaos of hugs and tears. "I'm so glad to see you, Granny! Thank you so much for coming to see me,"

Cindy said as she hugged her grandmother, tears streaming down her face. They walked toward Cindy's room, leaving the officer and lady standing in the entranceway.

*****

"Oh, that smells great," Darcy said as Steve entered her room with peach cobbler on the wooden tray.

"I hope you like it. I stood in line for all of ten minutes at the bakery down the street to get it especially for you after Granny left with Officer Riddle to go visit Cindy."

The mention of her name caused Darcy to tense, and she felt anger grow inside of her. *I know it's not really her fault my Dillon is gone. Why do I still blame her?* "I'm sure I will. I really appreciate all you're doing to take care of me and Hope," she said as she took the tray from Steve.

"I'd like to invite my granny over for dinner tomorrow if that's okay with you. She said she has something really important to discuss with me while she's here."

"No, that's fine," she said but didn't sound happy about it. Darcy silently prayed and began eating her dinner. Without another word, Steve left the room in search of Hope.

# CHAPTER 30

*H*eavenly Father, thank you for blessing me with this little one. *Please help me, I'm so hurt and angry right now. I can't believe You took my Dillon away from me. Please help me. I can't do this alone. I'm so hurt and angry. Angry at You for taking him,* Darcy prayed as she snuggled down to take a nap before dinner.

\*\*\*\*\*

Steve paced the front porch, staring at the downpour. He knew it wouldn't last long; it never did in Charleston. He kept watching the street hoping his granny wouldn't be late. Pausing from his restless pacing, Steve wondered if this was a good idea. He knew it would cause stress for Darcy, but he didn't know another way to take care of Darcy and hear what his granny had to tell him before she returned to Greenville. Steve breathed a sigh of relief as the rental car pulled in front of the house and she got out.

Steve decided to meet her on the walkway, anxious to hear what she had to say and hear how his sister was doing.

"How are you?" Granny asked as she grabbed his arm and continued walking toward the house.

"I'm fine, Granny. How are you today?"

"Oh, these old bones are doing just fine. The good Lord has blessed me with another day, so I can't complain," she said as he opened the door for them.

"Have a seat in the living room. Are you ready for dinner?" he asked as he turned the television on.

"Yes, I am."

"Do you mind if we watch the news while we eat, and then we can talk?" he asked. Granny nodded and moved to turn the volume up. Steve shook his head and placed a silencing finger to his lips as he pointed toward Darcy's room. "She's taking a nap," he said as he disappeared into the kitchen.

"How about some supper?" he asked Hope as she emerged from her room and joined him.

The soft voices on the TV filled the living room as they enjoyed their dinner. When they finished, Steve told Hope to play quietly in her room.

"Granny, you said you had something to talk to me about," Steve said as he entered the living room with dessert.

"I do," she said as she took the bowl he offered her. "It's about when your parents were killed."

"Granny, I'd rather not talk about that if you don't mind. If they hadn't been so selfish by becoming missionaries, they would've been home taking care of their children and wouldn't have been killed," Steve snapped as his voice tightened and a knot threatened to choke him.

"Honey, your parents loved you more than anything. Even though they dedicated their lives to telling others about Jesus, they always had your best interest in mind."

"Yeah, right."

"That's what I wanted to talk to you about tonight," she continued. "Your parents invested what little money they had in a stock called Duke Power, and the stock has risen tremendously."

"Granny, what are you trying to tell me?" Steve asked.

"All the money they invested is for you and Cindy. I forgot about it until I started cleaning out the back room. I found it among some papers and called the company. The stock is worth a little over $750,000."

Steve's eyes never left his grandmother's face as he sank further into his chair, unable to say a word as the information she just dumped on him sank in. Silence filled the living room once again. His voice took on a dreamy quality as he said, "Seven hundred fifty thousand dollars, wow!"

"Honey, you're the beneficiary of the policy," she said, bringing him back to reality.

"Granny, I can't believe it. I've been so worried about whether to reenlist or finally pursue my dream. I honestly thought I'd never be able to make my dream come true," Steve's voice trailed off as he became lost in his thoughts of the future. Without saying a word, Steve walked from the living room into the kitchen, mechanically cleaning the mess from dinner as his mind played thought after thought of all the things he could do with the money.

Once the kitchen was clean, he returned to the living room. "I'm so sorry, Granny," he said as he shook his head, still having trouble believing the wonderful news she shared with him. "I'm sorry I'm not much company tonight. I just have a lot to think about. Granny, this will really change my life," he said as reached and hugged the precious lady beside him.

"I know, honey. You're a great man, and I know you'll do the right thing for you and Cindy with it," she said as she covered her mouth to hide the escaping yawn. "I really need to get back to Cindy. The director said I could stay the night with her. It's been a long day and I'm tired."

"Of course," he said as he rose and helped her to her feet. They walked to the door and talked a little while longer. "Tell Cindy I love her and will see her whenever they'll allow me."

"I will," she said as she stepped onto the front porch and retrieved the keys from her purse. Steve bent to kiss her silver-blue tinged hair, which barely covered her head. "I love you, Granny. I have always loved you," he told her while holding her in his arms as if afraid to let go. "I hope you know you'll never want for anything. I'll always take care of you."

She smiled warmly. She patted his hand and kissed him on the cheek before she made her way to the car and headed back to the safe house to spend some time with Cindy.

# CHAPTER 31

The gentle glow of dawn filtered through the curtains of Darcy's room. Each new day only added to her sadness and pain. *Lord, You could have saved him, but for some reason, You chose to take him home. I'll never understand why You allowed this to happen to us, especially with this little one growing inside. Why, Lord? Why?* She lay in her bed, wiping the continuous flow of tears with one hand and the other gently holding the small rounding of her stomach. "I can't endure this!" she screamed as she looked at the ceiling, not hearing the door to her bedroom open.

"Darcy, are you okay?" Steve asked as walked into her room with a tray of coffee, orange juice, and muffins. He set the tray on the table beside her bed and knelt so he could look into her eyes. "Darcy, when I came in, you said you couldn't endure this any longer. Are you in pain?"

She slowly rose, propping herself against the headboard before reaching for the cup of coffee on her nightstand. She couldn't hide the gnawing emptiness inside her heart, a festering grief devouring her soul. "It's hard to believe he's gone. I keep waiting for him to call and say he'll be home soon or for him to come through the door and drop onto the sofa after a difficult day at work," she said as she stared past Steve, lost in her own thoughts.

Steve watched in silence as Darcy gripped the steaming cup, eyes filled with tears on the verge of spilling down her tired-looking

152

red face. He reached and touched her arm. "I'll leave you to your breakfast. Is there anything I can do to help you get ready for today?" he asked, almost in a whisper.

*Today, my sweet, sweet husband's funeral.* All she could manage was a shake of her head. Steve rose and left the room, closing the door behind him. Darcy sat reflecting on the family that now would never be. *Lord, this isn't the way I wanted my life to be,* she thought.

*Seek me, child. I'll take care of your wants and needs.* Darcy closed her eyes, absorbing the voice in her head trying to comfort her.

*I don't want to seek you! I want Dillon!* she cried as she leaned against the headboard.

*****

Tears welled in Darcy's eyes as she moved toward the copper box. Half of the box was open, allowing her to see her precious Dillon's face. The other half was draped with a white linen and topped with a single sunflower and red rose.

*"Happy birthday, darling,"* he had said as he handed her the small vase with a single sunflower and red rose. *"The sunflower reminds me you are the sunshine of my life and the rose represents my love for you."* The memory unlocked the floodgate that held back the tears.

Darcy stopped and turned toward Steve who tightened his grip on her arm as he escorted her toward the casket. "Oh Steve, why, why did God take him?" she asked as she buried her face into his chest and sobbed.

"Darcy, I don't know why this happened, but I'm here to help you through it," he said as he handed her a handkerchief and led her toward the end of the aisle.

With a faltering breath, Darcy stopped. She wiped her eyes and leaned down, pausing only inches from Dillon's face. The scent of the sunflower and rose reminded her of brighter days as she smoothed the stray hair from his forehead. "Oh honey, your face is as smooth and cold as the beautiful porcelain doll you gave me our first Christmas together," she whispered as her fingers traced the familiar lines of his face. *Our last Christmas together, our last everything together.* The thought grabbed her, and she felt as if someone punched her in the stomach and found it difficult to breathe. She needed to sit down. Before she could turn to find a seat, Steve was beside her with a chair and cool, wet cloth. "Oh, Dillon, I love you and I miss you so much. Why did you have to leave me? Why did you leave us?" she yelled as Steve guided her to the seat and wiped her face with the rag. *Lord, you promised to never desert us, even in the midst of a storm. Why aren't You here with me now? Why have You deserted me and my child? Why?*

"Can I get you anything?" Steve asked as he leaned toward her so only she could hear.

"The only thing I need is my husband, and you can't bring him back," she snapped as she pulled the rag from his hands and covered her face.

"Are you going to be able to sit beside the casket and greet your friends and family?" Steve asked. "I can talk with the pastor. I'm sure there's a private room somewhere you could sit until time for the service."

"I have to be here, Steve. I can't leave Dillon now. This is the last time I'll ever be able to be this close to him. I miss him so much. Why did he leave me?"

Silence filled the room. Steve placed his hand on her shoulder and looked into her eyes. "If there's anything I can do for you, let me know, and I'll take care of it." Darcy nodded, never taking her eyes off the dark-haired man she called her prince charming now lying in the cold metal box at the front of the church.

*****

Darcy reached out and shook hand after hand. She could hear everyone telling her how sorry they were and to call if she needed anything, but the words floated past her ears to be lost in space forever. Faces passed by in a blur but seemed to never end. She was grateful when Pastor Watson stood before her with his warm, compassionate smile.

"Darcy, why don't you sit over here on the pew, and I'll begin the service." Without another word, Darcy rose from the chair. Steve took her arm and led her to the pew.

"Let's pray," Pastor Watson said as he began the service. "Lord, we come to You with heavy hearts. Hearts which are broken and hurt by the tragic, shocking death of Dr. Collins. We know nothing catches You by surprise, and Dillon is now with You singing Your praises, but it still leaves the ones left behind to carry on with the pain of missing such a caring, loving man. We thank you, Lord, for the time You blessed us with Dillon here on earth. Help us lean on You, Lord, and give us comfort and wisdom as we deal with this terrible loss. In Your son's precious name, Amen."

Darcy's hands shook like leaves on a tree blowing in the midst of a storm. She felt she was on the edge of the deepest, darkest canyon and the only thing keeping her from tumbling over the edge was the slight flutter in her midsection. She forced herself to take several deep breaths. *Lord, I want so badly to be with Dillon. Why? Why is he gone?* she sighed and folded her hands, placing them in her lap. *Lord, give me strength to get through this,* she begged but continued to feel helpless, hopeless.

# CHAPTER 32

One week later, Darcy studied the pretty girl who was typically full of life. Her delicate features were enhanced by her penetrating green eyes, a striking contrast to her curly ebony hair. "Would you like some company?" she asked as she entered Hope's room.

Hope turned, tears flowing freely from her eyes, and she ran to Darcy's waiting arms.

Darcy embraced the girl and stroked her back. "Sshh, it'll be okay."

Hope's lower lip quivered. "It's, it's just not fair," she said between sobs.

Darcy laid her head atop the little one still wrapped in her arms. "I know it's not fair. Sometimes, life's really hard," she said as she lowered herself to her knees. Placing a hand under Hope's chin, she gently raised her face so she could peer into her eyes. "Hope, God never promised us life would be easy, but He did promise He would never leave us." *Lord, help me remember that too.* "Dillon used to tell me no matter what we faced in life, we'll never be alone. He used to say between the three of us we would be okay."

"The three of you?"

Darcy brushed away the tears streaming down the little girl's face and smiled as she remembered Dillon reassuring her during difficult times. "Dillon was talking about me, him, and God. He said no matter what we faced in life, there'd always be the three of us to face it together." Silence filled the room. *Dillon, you lied to me. You left me and now I'm alone.* Darcy was lost in thought when the tugging on her shirt sleeve brought her back to Hope's room. "I'm sorry, honey. I was thinking about something else. What did you say?"

Hope blinked her weepy eyes. "Now I know why God took my mommy and daddy to heaven."

Perplexed by her statement, Darcy stood, took Hope by the hand, and walked to her bed. She sat on the bed and placed Hope in her lap. "Why do you think God took your mommy and daddy to heaven?"

"He took them to heaven so when God wanted Dillon to come to heaven, you'd still have three to help you through things—you, God, and me," she said matter-of-factly.

Darcy decided not to bring up the letter she received from the Department of Social Services. She didn't have the heart to add another painful goodbye to the little girl's life. At least not today.

*****

"Okay, Darcy, back to bed," he said as he laid Hope in her bed.

"I'm fine, Steve," she said as she bent to pick up the teddy bear left in the floor by the closet door.

"No, ma'am. The doctor said you needed complete bed rest until your little one is born. You've been on your feet the last few days, and I'm worried about you," he said as he took the teddy bear and laid it on the bed beside Hope. He then gently guided her from Hope's room, down the hall, and stopped at Darcy's bedroom door. "Now, I know this is a very difficult time for you and that's even more of a reason you should be in bed. You've made it through the funeral, and things are starting to settle down a little. It's time for you to take care of yourself and the little one you're carrying," he said with no room for debate as he opened her door. "Now, are you going to get dressed for bed and let me take care of you and Hope, or do I need to dress you myself?" he asked as a smirk covered his face.

"Okay, bossy. I'm going. I can dress myself, thank you," she snipped playfully as she walked into her room and shut the door.

"I'll be back in ten minutes with a snack and to make sure you're in bed," he said through the closed door.

A faint smile covered Darcy's face. *It's nice having someone here to help me right now. I'm really glad he's here.*

*****

Steve and Hope were busy in the kitchen mixing their secret recipe for pancakes. "Now you have to promise you'll never share our secret ingredient which makes these pancakes light and fluffy," he said as he handed her the big wooden spoon so she could stir the batter.

"I'll never tell. I promise, Mr. Steve," she said as a smile covered her face and she struggled to mix the batter.

They continued their mission until everything was complete. "Okay, if you'll grab the syrup, we'll set it on the tray and take it to Mrs. Darcy," he said as he grinned at the animated dark-haired moppet as she stretched and reached for the syrup that sat inches from her grasp. "Here, let me help you," he placed the bottle on the tray, and they carried it to Darcy's room.

"Can I open the door?" she asked.

"Let's knock—" Hope opened the door before he could finish his reply, and Hope bounced into the room.

"Good morning!" she said as she hopped onto the bed beside Darcy. "Look what we made."

"I see," she said as a smile illuminated her face. "I was wondering what all the noise was I heard coming from the kitchen."

Steve placed the tray over Darcy's lap and picked up the excited bundle sitting beside her, chatting away. "We're going to clean up the kitchen and get ready. I'll come back in about thirty minutes and get the tray," he said. He set Hope down, and she ran toward her room. "Do you still feel up to talking with Hope about the letter you received from DSS?"

Darcy slowly shook her head, and a sadness filled her eyes. "No, not really, but I can't wait much longer."

"Well, I know she's going to be upset. I hate that she may be uprooted just as she seems to be adjusting well. Are you sure this is the right thing to do for her?"

"No, I'm not, but I don't have a choice. I'm not her legal guardian. I'm just her foster mom," she said as she put another bite of pancakes into her mouth.

"I'll let you eat. We can discuss this after I finish the dishes." He turned and closed the door. Solutions for this dilemma raced through his mind.

*****

After a sleepless night, Steve rose early. Once he took Darcy her breakfast, he returned to the kitchen for some quiet time while Hope was still sleeping. He stared at the dishes drying in the rack as he wiped his hands on the damp dishtowel. *What in the world's going to happen to Hope? What can I do to help her and Darcy? Why can't they leave the sweet little girl alone? She's been through enough in her short time here on Earth.* He heard steps pitter-patter across the hardwood floors in the living room and turned his head just in time to see Hope enter the kitchen, yawning and rubbing her eyes. "Good morning, sleepyhead," he said as he squatted and patted her disheveled hair. "I just carried Mrs. Darcy some eggs and bacon. Would you like some?"

Hope nodded and climbed onto the chair at the kitchen table. Steve busied himself, fighting back the fear as thoughts of Hope's future ran through his head. Minutes later, he turned with a small princess plate filled with scrambled eggs and bacon. "Here, sweetie, eat your breakfast, and after you eat, I'll help you get dressed. We have a visitor coming in a little while." Without a word, Hope began eating, and Steve took the opportunity to leave the kitchen before she could see the tears escape from his eyes. He entered the bathroom and washed his face. *Pull it together, Steve. These girls need you. Besides, no matter what happens, it doesn't really affect you.* He shook his head as if trying to erase his thoughts and the situation they must face in a few hours. Walking quietly to Darcy's door, he deeply inhaled and slowly exhaled. Once at the door, he gently knocked.

"Come in."

The door creaked as he pushed it open just enough to stick his head in. "How are you feeling this morning?" he asked as he looked at the empty plate on Darcy's tray and smiled. "I'm glad to see your appetite's coming back."

"Yeah, me too," she said as she sat the tray on the mattress beside her. "I'm having a really tough time this morning. I know we need to talk with Hope before Mrs. Evans comes over this morning."

Steve shook his head in agreement, unable to find the words to comfort or encourage her.

"Is she up?"

He tipped his head back and closed his eyes, finding it difficult to fight the urge to just disappear with the two of them and start life anew. "She's in the kitchen eating breakfast. I'll help her get ready when she's done."

"I appreciate your help," she said.

Noticing she seemed stressed, Steve thought it would be best to get this conversation over with. "Maybe we should go ahead and talk with Hope. Sort of prepare her for this afternoon."

"Prepare me for what?" Hope asked as she walked into Darcy's room and climbed onto the bed, snuggling next to Darcy. Darcy covered her with the blanket and stroked her head.

Steve and Darcy exchanged looks, neither of them saying a word. Steve walked over and sat on the foot of the bed facing the girls. "Hope, there's a lady coming to visit this afternoon." He paused, searching for an easy way to say what he knew had to be said. "Honey, Mrs. Darcy and I love you very much, and no matter what this lady has to say, you need to remember that, okay?

Hope tilted her head and knitted her brows as she looked at Steve. "Okay," she slowly said. "Why is she coming here?"

Darcy exhaled and pulled Hope closer. "She's coming by to check on you and to talk to us about you living here."

Before anyone could say anything else, Hope jumped from the bed, placed her hands on her hips, and shrieked as tears ran down her cheeks, "Don't you want me anymore?"

"Yes, yes," Darcy said as her voice tightened, and a knot threatened to cut off her air supply. "Of course, we do."

"Then why is she coming to talk to me about living here? Is she going to take me away?"

"No, honey. Not if I can help it," Darcy said, her voice much softer. "See, baby, I'm your foster mom, and she wants to talk with us about a home you can stay in forever. A home where you'll never have to leave again."

"Why can't I stay here?"

"I'm hoping you can, but I want you to be prepared in case she has other plans." Darcy reached out for the little girl, but Hope pulled out of her reach. "Hope, please, try to understand. I don't have any control over child services. I'm going to do everything I can to keep you here with me."

Tears were freely flowing down Hope's precious cheeks, and her lips were pursed in a full pout. "Why would she make me leave here if you want me?"

"Hope, I would need to adopt you for you to stay here, and in order to do that, I'd have to meet their guidelines."

"Why can't you meet their guidelines? Don't you want me? Do you love me?"

"Honey, it's not that simple. Of course, I want you and I love you and want you to stay with me."

"Then why can't I stay?"

Steve stood and swooped Hope into his arms. "Hope, Mrs. Darcy wants you to stay, and she loves you very much. When you were sent here to live with Mrs. Darcy, they thought Mrs. Darcy and her husband might adopt you and you'd stay here forever. Since Mrs. Darcy's husband isn't here, and Mrs. Darcy can't take care of you until her baby is born, they're worried about you."

Hope peered into Steve's eyes and placed her hands on either side of his cheeks. "Then why can't you be Mrs. Darcy's husband and then adopt me?"

Steve kissed her on the forehead and set her on the floor. At a loss for words, the room was filled with silence, which was broken as Hope screamed she wouldn't go and ran to her room.

*****

Hope sat huddled in the middle of her bed. The silence was scary, like when she awoke after the wreck with her daddy. No matter how many times she called his name, there was no answer. But then a lot of things were scary at her young age. The doorbell echoed in the distance. Hope gulped, praying it wasn't the mean lady trying to take her away. The house was quiet again, and Hope thought maybe she imagined the sound of the doorbell until there was a gentle rapping at her door. Hope pulled the covers over her head, trying to disappear. Her door squeaked open, and Steve walked in and eased onto the side of her bed.

"Hope, Mrs. Evans is here," he said as he placed his hand on the lump in the covers.

Hope didn't move, hoping if she were still enough, he'd go away.

"Come on, honey. Let's go talk to her and see what we can work out."

Reluctantly, she lowered the covers, her eyes wide with fear. Without a word, she moved to his arms. He pulled her close and held her in a tight hug for a few moments before standing and carrying her to the living room. Once they entered the room, he sat in the chair across from Mrs. Evans with Hope still on his lap. "Hope, this is Mrs. Evans, and she has a few questions for you."

Mrs. Evans smiled at Hope and began explaining to her the reason she was there. As she kept talking, Hope stared blankly at her, her little mind racing with thoughts of this strange lady taking her away and giving her to strangers. Not a single word the lady said was heard by Hope. Suddenly, Hope jumped from Steve's lap. Overcome by fear and anxiety, she ran to her room crying. "I don't want to leave Mrs. Darcy and Mr. Steve. If you try to make me, I'll run away forever," she yelled as she shut the door to her room. She huddled under her bed, her body heaving with sobs until sleep lured her into the peaceful darkness.

*****

"I'm sorry, Mrs. Evans," Darcy said as the lady rose to leave. "I love Hope and have every intention to adopt her."

"Mrs. Collins, I'm well aware of your intentions to adopt Hope, and the adoption was in progress until the loss of your husband," she said as she peered at Darcy over the square dark-framed glasses on her nose. "When your husband passed away…"

"Was murdered!" Darcy snapped, correcting the rigid woman standing before her. "He was murdered. He didn't pass away. Besides, his death doesn't change my love for Hope."

Unflinching, Mrs. Evans continued, "As I was saying, since your husband's death, the state won't allow a single woman to adopt a child. It's our desire to place her with loving parents or a group home. It's highly unlikely you'd be eligible to keep her on a permanent basis unless you were running a group home. You're welcome to continue to foster her if you wish. At least, until suitable arrangements can be made."

"Thank you, Mrs. Evans. I'll talk with Darcy about her options and get back to you soon," Steve said as he stood and opened the front door, ending their conversation and queuing her to leave. "Darcy needs her rest and definitely doesn't need the additional stress you introduced today. I'm sure we'll find a solution to this issue." Without another word, Mrs. Evans picked up her satchel and left the home. Once she was out the door, Steve shut and locked it behind her. "Darcy, why don't you go lie down, and I'll check on Hope and make some lunch."

"Oh, Steve," Darcy said as tears burst from her eyes and her body shook with sobs. "What am I going to do? I love her and don't want to lose her."

Steve pulled Darcy into his arms and held her as she cried on his shoulder. "I'm not sure, but I won't let you lose her. I have an idea I'd like to talk to you about, so why don't you lie down for a little while. I'll check on Hope, and we'll bring you lunch soon. After lunch, while Hope's watching *Sesame Street*, I'll come and talk with you about my plan."

She nodded, wiping her eyes with her hand and walked toward the bedroom. Steve accompanied her to the door. Once she was in her room, he shut her door and went to check on Hope.

*****

Hope grabbed the bread from the counter as Steve gathered the ham and cheese from the refrigerator. Hope placed two slices of bread on each plate. As Steve laid ham on one side of each sandwich, Hope placed a piece of cheese on the other slice of bread. Once the bread slices were set on top of each other, they added chips to the plates.

"I'll carry the tray. Can you carry all three bottles of water?" Steve asked as Hope wrapped the bottles securely in her arms. Smiling at her efforts, he winked at her and nodded toward the door. "Okay, let's go take this to Mrs. Darcy, and we'll have a picnic in her bedroom." His heart melted as her eyes beamed with delight and a smile covered her face. Together, they carried their treasures to Darcy's room. Steve tapped on the door. "Are you ready for lunch?" he asked before easing the door open. Before Darcy could answer, Hope skipped into the room, dropping one of the unopened water bottles.

Darcy laughed at the sight of the two entering her room. "It's okay, sweetie. Hop up here with me," she said as she patted the mattress beside her.

Steve set the tray on the nightstand and bent to pick up the bottle of water. "We thought we'd picnic in here with you for lunch, if you don't mind."

"I'd love it," she answered with a happiness in her voice Steve hadn't heard for a while. The three of them sat and ate as they listened to Hope describe the latest escapades of Sylvester and Tweety Bird.

Once they finished lunch, Steve rose and gathered the dishes. "I'll give you ladies some girl time while I clean the kitchen," he said, smiling at the sight of Hope snuggling next to Darcy. The girls lay face-to-face as Hope's animated story continued. He quietly closed the door as he headed for the kitchen. He finished dishes as quickly as he could.

Excited over what he thought was the perfect solution, Steve hurried back to Darcy's door when he was done cleaning. He gently knocked and eased the door open. Before he could say a word, he was greeted with Darcy's index finger placed upon her lips, and his eyes followed hers as they looked down at the sleeping dark-haired angel snuggled close to Darcy. Feeling a little deflated, Steve nodded his head in understanding. "I'll come back when she's awake," he whispered and eased the door shut.

\*\*\*\*\*

Steve awoke to the sound of the laughing bird as Hope turned on the television to watch *Woody Woodpecker*. Taking a few moments to gather his bearings and fully wake up, he lay on the couch and watched as Hope sat mesmerized by the characters on the screen. His plan to keep Darcy and Hope together floated through his mind, and he smiled as he rose from the couch and sat beside Hope on the floor. Her eyes never left the screen. "Sweetie, sit here and watch your cartoons. I'm going to talk with Mrs. Darcy and will be back in a little while," he said as she nodded in agreement. Not sure if she heard him, he patted the top of her head, stood up, and headed toward Darcy's room.

Her door was still open from when Hope left moments ago. Steve stuck his head in, and once he saw she was awake and reading a book, he took a step into her room. "Hey, do you feel like talking for a little while? I have an idea which may help you and Hope."

Darcy turned to face him as she set her book on the table beside her bed. "Sure, come on in."

Steve walked to the chair at her bedside and sat down. "Please, hear me out before you say anything."

She nodded.

"I know the state wants Hope with an adoptive family or in a group home, and I have an idea where you'll be taken care of with your little one coming, Hope can stay with you, and you can do all of this and stay at home with the children and not have to worry about work."

Darcy knit her eyebrows and pursed her lips. Her words were slow and hesitant. "How in the world do you think I could manage that? I'll have to work after the baby's born to make ends meet. My savings and the life insurance won't last forever," she said as she tilted her head and stared at Steve like he'd lost his mind.

"I know, but we haven't had much time to talk about my visit with my granny with everything else going on."

"What does your visit with your granny have to do with me and Hope?"

"Well, I'm not sure how to begin," he said as he paused to find the right words. Darcy sat quietly on the bed, amusement dancing across her face. "Before my parents were murdered, they made an investment. While cleaning up her house, my granny found the paperwork regarding the investment. To make a long story short, I'm the beneficiary of it, and I'd like to help you," he explained as he leaned forward, placing his elbows on his knees and propping his chin in his hand.

"I don't understand how an investment your parents made is going to help me keep Hope. They want her with a couple or in a group home."

Realizing he forgot to explain how he wanted to help her, he straightened in the chair and reached for her hand. Once he was holding her hand, he tried to explain again. "I'd like to finish building the plans for this house for you, your little one, and Hope." Not giving her a chance to ask questions, he continued. "I can build the house to code for a group home. I could have a separate living quarter and take care of maintenance, the yard work, and provide the children with guidance as a male role model. The children would have their own rooms, and you would be not only your little one's mom but the caretaker for Hope. We can register the home with DSS and make it a business. With it being a private business and not a government-run business, you can decide how many children you want to keep in the home."

Darcy sat stunned, unable to respond.

"I know it's a lot to think about, but please think about it and let me know if it's something you'd like to do."

Tears began to slide down her cheeks. "Steve, I don't know what to say. That plan may work, but I can't ask you to spend your money for something like that. Do you know how much a DSS-regulated home costs?"

"Look, I have no responsibilities other than my sister and granny. The money is more than enough, and besides, I have the money I've saved from my years in the Navy. I can take care of the financial part if you can take care of yourself and the children. Besides, I've grown fond of the little scamp."

"I don't know what to say. It's such a selfless and generous offer."

"Say yes," he said as his face beamed with excitement.

Nodding her head with tears flowing, she said yes.

Steve stood, bent down, and gave her a hug. "I'll start planning the details, and we can start construction right away. You can make the decisions for the work right here in your bed."

"I can't wait," she said.

"While I'm working on plans for the renovations, why don't you call DSS and let them know of our plans. If they are satisfied with the idea, and Hope can stay, we can sit down with her tonight after dinner and give her the news," he said as he stood by her door. Without needing any further prompting, Darcy picked up the phone and was dialing the number on the card before he could leave the room.

# CHAPTER 33

*One week later*

"Hey Darcy, it's great to see you again. I'm so sorry about Dillon. I've been praying for you," Ed said as he entered the room.

A faint smile creeped across Darcy face as she pulled the familiar pink paper cover a little tighter around her chest. "Thank you. I appreciate the prayers."

"Let's check on the little one here," he said as he started his examination. The room was quiet as he threw the rubber gloves into the trash, picked up the folder on the table across the room and began writing. "Hmm," he said as he sat on the stool by the exam table.

Darcy sat up, her eyes fixed on the man in the white lab coat. "Ed, is everything all right?" she asked, her voice tight with concern.

He slowly looked up from his notes. His eyes peered into hers, and silence filled the air. "Darcy, I'm really concerned about your blood pressure."

"I'm doing everything you told me to do. I'm always in bed when I'm home, and I'm watching my salt intake," she said, trying to ease his concerns.

"Well, it's not just your blood pressure. There was a good bit of protein in your urine. I know you're under a great deal of stress. Have you been having headaches or nausea lately?"

Darcy tilted her head and squinted her eyes. Nodding her head, she said, "Yeah, but aren't those symptoms part of being pregnant?"

"Sometimes," he said as he reviewed his notes again. "But, you're only sixteen weeks, and I'm worried about your health and the health of your little one. To be safe, I'd like to give you a prescription for medicine to lower your blood pressure."

Darcy nodded her head in agreement as she took the blue piece of paper from him. "I'll get it filled on my way home."

"Darcy, I'd really like to admit you to the hospital until—"

"No!" Darcy snapped, sterner than she intended. "I can't be hospitalized. I have too much to do. DSS is coming at the end of the week, and Hope needs me."

"I understand, believe me. I'm just worried about the baby," he said as he placed his hand on her shoulder. "Look, let's give the medicine time to work. If you'll promise to stay in bed and see me in two weeks, maybe we can get things under control."

She smiled as she thanked him for the compromise. *The baby will be okay. Surely, God wouldn't take it too.*

*****

"Hey Granny," Cindy said as she hurried to the sweet woman, wrapping her arms around her neck as she entered the door.

"Hey, honey. It's so good to see you."

"Oh, Granny, I've missed you so much. I'll be glad when I can come home," she said as her grandmother returned her hug, and they walked to the sofa in the common room. "Is your luggage in the car?" she asked, sitting beside her granny.

"Yes, it's in the back seat. I'll get it later. I'm a little tired from the drive."

"Don't be silly, I'll go get your luggage. Why don't you go to my room and lay down?" she said as she stood, took the keys from her granny, and walked toward the car. Her granny did as Cindy suggested. By the time Cindy came back with the luggage, her granny was lying on the bed, her eyes closed. Not sure if she were praying or asleep, Cindy left the bags beside the door.

*****

"Get up," the officer barked as he opened the cell door.

Michael sat up from the steel bed covered with a thin mat. "What?"

"You need to shower and start preparing for your court appearance," the officer said as he threw a towel in Michael's direction.

Michael didn't flinch as the towel landed at his feet. "I don't need to do nuthin'. The way I look ain't gonna make any difference. You guys are all the same. If you want someone in jail, there's nothing they can do to stop it. I hope you're happy putting an innocent man behind bars."

"It's not up to me to determine if you're guilty or not. That's between you, your attorney, the judge, and jury. I'm just making sure justice is served," he said as he turned to leave the cell. "Your attorney will be here in an hour to go over your case. You have court in a couple of weeks. If you change your mind about the shower, you'll have to wait until tonight. I have other things to do than try to make you clean yourself up."

The clanging of the door was the last word Michael heard. He sat on the bed staring down at the ragged towel that sat at his feet. *Why am I here? Don't they know I can't help the things I do when I drink?*

*****

"Steve?" Darcy yelled from her room as she heard the front door close.

"Yea," he said. "I'll be there in a minute. Let me put the groceries down," he replied as he walked into the kitchen.

Hope ran toward Darcy's room when she realized Darcy was awake. Without hesitation, she opened her door, ran into her room, and jumped onto the bed. "Hey, Mrs. Darcy. How are you feeling?"

A smile covered Darcy's face and danced in her eyes as she watched the little girl bounce onto the bed but gently approach her tummy as if she would bother the baby. "I'm good, sweetie. I have some great news, but I need to wait for Mr. Steve to come in so I can tell him too."

"Mr. Steve, hurry!" Hope yelled.

Hearing the commotion, Steve sat the bags onto the kitchen table. He didn't bother putting them away. He hurried toward the room where the two girls were giggling. As he entered the room, he noticed Darcy had Hope snuggled beside her. "What's all the excitement about?"

Darcy sat up straighter in the bed. She pulled Hope into her lap and motioned for Steve to sit on the bed. After he was comfortably sitting at the foot of the bed, she smiled. "I heard from Mary with DSS," she said and paused. Her eyes locked with Steve. Hope leaned closer to Darcy.

"Well?" Steve asked, anxious to hear what had her so excited.

"She approved the plans we submitted," Darcy said as she clasped her hands together.

Steve's eye widened. He stood from the bed, and a smile stretched across his face, almost reaching ear to ear. "That's wonderful!" he exclaimed.

Confused, Hope hopped from the bed. She pulled on Steve's shirt sleeve. "What's going on?" she asked.

"Oh, Hope!" Darcy squealed with excitement. "It means you get to stay here with us. It means no one will take you away."

Overcome with happiness, Hope jumped back onto the bed and threw herself into Darcy's arms. The girls were embracing when the words Darcy just said to Hope sunk into Steve's thoughts. *You get to stay here with us...us.* "I need to put the groceries away. I'll bring you some lunch shortly," he said and quickly left.

*****

"Are you feeling better?" Cindy asked as her granny emerged from the bedroom after her nap.

"Yes, I am. Thank you," she said as she entered the kitchen, taking the seat beside her granddaughter.

"I made some spaghetti for lunch. Would you like some?" Cindy asked.

"Sure. I'd love some," she said. "Are you ready for the hearing?" Granny asked.

Cindy's heart lurched as she was reminded of the hearing. She paused, inhaled deeply. She slowly exhaled as she finished preparing her granny's plate. "I guess. I really don't understand how they can charge someone for something they had no control over," she said as she set the plate down. "I need to get something from my room," she said and left before her granny could respond.

# CHAPTER 34

*Five weeks later*

"Good morning," Steve said as he walked into Darcy's room with a tray of muffins and juice. "I know you want to go this morning, but I really wish you'd stay here. You know I'll tell you everything that happens."

"I know," she said, taking the tray from him. "I can't stay here. He can't take anything else away from me. Besides, I want to look him in the eyes. I want him to know, he may have killed my husband, but he can't defeat me," she said as she popped a piece of muffin into her mouth.

Steve sat on the bed beside her. "I know it's important for you, Darcy. I'm just worried about the baby. Besides, something could happen like it did a few weeks ago. His hearing could be rescheduled again, and we could go for nothing," he said as he watched her drink the juice to wash down the muffin.

After a few moments, she wiped her mouth and looked at him. "I know and I really appreciate everything you do to help me. But I have to go."

Knowing this was a battle he wouldn't win, Steve stood and walked toward the door. "Okay," he said, turning to face her before he left the room. "I'll be back in about an hour for the tray. I'll get

173

ready, then I'll take Hope to Pastor Watson. He said he'd watch her while we're in court."

"Thank you," she said as he shut the door.

*****

"You look beautiful," Granny said as Cindy emerged from the bathroom. "How do you feel?"

Smoothing the front of her skirt, Cindy looked in the mirror. The black and blue that covered her face had disappeared, but the emotional scars were still raw. "I'm okay, Granny. I just don't know what to do. I still love him. Why can't they see he can't help what he does when he drinks?" she asked, sitting on the bed as tears began to fall.

"Cindy, he's an alcoholic and needs professional help," Granny said as she took her granddaughter's hand into hers. "You're such a loving person. I know you're torn in your heart, but, honey, love doesn't hurt. God doesn't want you in a relationship where you're mistreated."

"God?" she asked. "Where was God when Dr. Collins was hurt? Where was God when I was being slapped and kicked? Where was God when my parents were killed doing His work?"

"Cindy, you know He is everywhere. I understand you're hurting and confused, but God never left you. He's always been with you," Granny explained as she stood and walked to the dresser, picking up her Bible. "People make decisions, and sometimes, those decisions affect others. It's not God's fault innocent people get hurt. It's man who's evil. Man's evil nature is why God sent His Son, Jesus, to die for our sins. He loves His children," she said as she opened the Bible, flipping through the pages.

Cindy sat quietly, dazed as memories of her parents, Michael's actions, and the way the doctor looked as she left him on the tarp in the middle of nowhere hopped through her mind. She was lost in thought when her granny shook her shoulder. "Did you hear what I said?" she asked as Cindy returned her attention to the lady beside her.

"No, Granny. I'm sorry. I was thinking about something else."

"I was saying, man has free choice, and sometimes those choices hurt others. In Matthew chapter 5 verse 45, it says, 'That ye may be the children of your Father which is in heaven: for He maketh His sun to rise on the evil and on the good, and sendth rain on the just and on the unjust.' See, honey, Michael's choice to drink to excess, causing him to lose control, is the reason Dr. Collins is no longer here. Michael's also responsible for hurting you."

"No, Granny. If I hadn't made him mad, he wouldn't have hit me," Cindy said, defending her husband.

"No, Cindy. Just because you make someone angry does not give them the right to hurt you. A real man never lays his hands on a woman, especially a woman he loves, in anger."

Tears filled Cindy's eyes as she realized her granny was right. No matter what she did or didn't do, as long as he was drinking, he would hurt her. "I guess you're right, Granny. If he really loved me, he wouldn't have hurt me," she said as she lowered her head and covered her face with her hands and cried.

The older woman pulled her close and held her. "I love you, Cindy. God loves you too."

"I know, Granny. I've been so far away from Him. I really want to be close to the Lord again."

"Honey, He's not the one who moved," Granny said in a soft whisper. "All you have to do is pray and ask Him to forgive you. He will forgive you. He always does," she said as Cindy wiped her eyes with a tissue from the box sitting on the table beside them.

"Granny, will you give me a few minutes? I'd like to pray," she asked as she stood. Her grandmother stood and walked toward the door as Cindy kneeled beside the bed. The door closed to give her privacy with her thoughts, prayers, and with the Lord.

*****

"Hey, Granny, Cindy," Steve said as he approached the two women walking toward him, hugging them both. "You can sit beside me if you'd like. I have a seat on the first bench," he said as he opened the heavy wooden door leading to the courtroom.

They followed him to the bench. He turned and motioned for them to have a seat. Once they were seated, he glanced around and noticed Darcy wasn't in the room. He started to leave to look for her, but the door opened, and Darcy entered the courtroom. She walked toward Steve; her eyes darted to the women sitting on the bench. *I wonder if that's her. The woman my husband went to help. The woman whose husband killed my Dillon.*

"Are you okay?" he asked as she stopped in front of him.

She nodded and looked at the women sitting on the bench, lost in their own conversation. "Is that your sister?"

"Yes, that's Cindy. I know you probably don't want her here, but she's here to testify for the prosecution. They'll be calling her out of the room before the trial starts," he said as he placed his hand at the small of her back and motioned for her to sit down. "Darcy, it's not her fault what her husband did. I'm sure she hates herself for what's happened."

Darcy sat on the bench, resting her hands on the swell of her stomach. She inhaled deeply and exhaled slowly. "I know," she said but did not look at Steve.

*I love you, My child. I also love her. You need to forgive her as I have forgiven you.* Darcy closed her eyes as the voice in her head continue to repeat thoughts of love and forgiveness.

Moments later, an officer approached the bench. Cindy rose and left the room with the officer. Darcy's heart began to pound, and her palms started to sweat. The door to the right of the judge's bench opened, and an officer entered the room and was followed by the man she assumed killed her husband. The two settled at the table to her left in front of the judge's bench. Before she could ask Steve about the scruffy man, a booming voice said, "All rise." Everyone in the courtroom stood as a gray-haired man in a black robe entered and took a seat at the judge's bench. The room was hot; Darcy's nausea threatened to make her spew. She could see the judge speaking but couldn't understand what he was saying as the room began to go dark.

*****

Darcy opened her eyes. It took her a moment to realize she was no longer in the courtroom. She blinked and focused on the man sitting beside her. "What happened?" she asked as their eyes met.

Steve placed his hand over hers. "You passed out. We're at the hospital. Your doctor is on the way."

"How long was I out?" she asked. Before he could answer, Ed came in.

"Well, young lady, you sure know how to keep a doctor on his toes," he said as he looked over the chart the nurse had handed him as he entered.

Darcy began to sit up but laid her head back as the room began to spin again.

"Your blood pressure is really high. You need to stay in bed," he said as he turned to the nurse and gave her some orders. When the nurse left, he turned to face Darcy. "I'm ordering IV beta blocker to decrease your heart rate. I also want to order—"

He was interrupted by Darcy's scream. "Oh, gosh. It hurts," she said as she grabbed her stomach.

"Get an external uterine monitor in here, STAT," he yelled as he put the stethoscope in his ears and placed the other end on her midsection. Moments later, she was hooked up to a machine strapped around her stomach. "Darcy, you're going into labor. I'm going to do everything I can to stop it. Whatever you do, don't push to the contractions. It's too early for this little one to be born," he told her as he turned to instruct the nurse of what he needed.

The nurse rushed from the room and returned shortly with a needle. "This needs to be injected in the back of your arm," she said as she approached the bed.

"What is it?" Darcy asked.

"It's Brethine," Ed said as the nurse injected it into Darcy's arm. "It's going to help slow the contractions. Hopefully, we can stop them." Once the medicine was in her arm, Ed sat in the chair beside her bed. After watching her for an hour, he patted her arm and stood beside her bed. "It looks like the medication is working and your contractions have stopped. I'm going to go get a coffee and will be back in about an hour. In the meantime, if you need anything, press the Call button and let the nurse know."

Darcy shook her head in agreement and watched as he left the room. Once he was gone, she turned to Steve and asked, "What happened in court?"

Steve stood and took the few steps to her bedside. "Darcy, you should really try to rest. Let's talk about court later."

"Steve, I need to know what happened."

Exhaling, Steve shook his head. "I didn't stay, I came here with you. According to my granny, about twenty minutes into the hearing, Michael stood up and interrupted his attorney. He told the judge he was guilty and was sorry. She said he told the judge he wasn't a bad person except when he's drinking. After several minutes, the judge accepted his guilty plea. According to my granny, the judge is supposed to sentence him in two weeks."

"That's wonderful," she said, wincing in pain as another contraction started.

Steve grabbed a washcloth and wet it with cold water. He placed it on her forehead. "You should really rest," he said as he bit his bottom lip and glanced around the room. "I think I'll go downstairs and get a coffee. Can I get you anything?"

"No, thank you. I'm really tired. I think I'll just try to get some sleep," she said.

A slight smile softened his scruffy face, and he nodded. "Okay. I'll be back shortly," he said, quietly walking out of the room. Once he was in the hall out of her view, he inhaled deeply. *Lord, if you really exist, Darcy and the little one need you right now. Please protect them and keep them safe.* Slowly he released his breath. *What in the world is happening to me? Here I am praying to a God I'm not sure exist. What power does this woman have over me?*

*****

Darcy opened her eyes when she heard the door open. "Did you get lost?" she asked. The words hung in the air as silence filled the room. She stared at her visitor, unsure what to say next. Moments passed as Cindy stood in the doorway holding a bouquet of flowers.

"I'm sorry to bother you. Please, can I talk with you for a moment?" Cindy asked as tears flowed down her cheeks.

Darcy's heart softened as she looked at the small woman standing in the doorway of her hospital room. She nodded her head and motioned for Cindy to take a seat next to the bed.

Cindy eased into the chair after setting the flowers on the bedside table. "I want to tell you how sorry I am about what happened to your husband."

Darcy gritted her teeth, her mind racing, searching for the right thing to say. *What do you expect from me? You're the reason my husband is dead.* Before she could say anything, her pastor's words from Sunday's sermon flooded her thoughts. *Christ loves everyone, even the worst sinner. He doesn't like the sin, but he loves the sinner. As Christians, we need to show others love and grace as Christ has shown us. How do you expect the lost to want to be saved if we show them anger and bitterness?* "I don't know what you want from me," Darcy said as she turned her head to face her visitor.

"I was worried about you and the baby. My grandmother has been praying for you and the little one. And I want you to know I'm so sorry that things turned out the way they have," Cindy said and continued before Darcy could reply. "Your husband was good to me and helped me many times when my husband would hit me after he had been drinking."

"Dillon was a wonderful man and would have been an amazing father if…" Darcy stopped midsentence as her door opened again.

"What are you doing here?" Steve barked as he entered the room and saw his sister sitting in the chair beside Darcy's bed.

"I came to apologize and ask Darcy to forgive me," Cindy said as Steve approached her and grabbed her by the arm.

"You need to leave. The last thing she needs right now is to deal with this mess," he said as Cindy rose from the chair to ease the grip he had on her.

"It's okay," Darcy said.

Steve stared at Darcy. "Are you sure?" he asked.

She nodded her head. "Yes, I'm sure. I'd like to hear what she has to say." *Where did that come from? Why do I care what this woman has to say? If she didn't call my husband, he'd be here today.*

"Thank you," Cindy said as she returned to her seat.

"Please, tell me what happened. I want to know everything," Darcy said as she adjusted herself in the bed. Steve walked to the other side of her and sat in the other chair.

Cindy began telling Darcy everything she could remember from the time Dr. Collins showed up at her house until the time they left him on the side of the road.

Darcy lay there, listening to every word as tears flowed from her eyes.

When Cindy finished, she laid her hands in her lap and looked at Darcy. "I wish I could do something to make things better, but I can't. I have learned at the safe house that it's not my fault Michael was abusive. I always felt if I had been a better person, he would treat me better. It was difficult for me to understand he's responsible for his actions. I want you to know, I'll do everything I can to help the prosecution with this case. Michael needs to face the consequences of his actions for a change instead of always getting away with whatever he does."

Darcy nodded her head. *Lord, what am I supposed to do here?* "I appreciate your help."

Cindy stood to leave. She grabbed the knob and opened the door. Before leaving, she turned and faced Darcy once again. "I hope you can find it in your heart to forgive me one day," she said and turned to go.

"Wait," Darcy said. "I do forgive you."

Cindy smiled as tears began to flow once again, and she silently left, closing the door behind her.

Steve stood and peered at Darcy. "Are you okay?"

Darcy nodded. "Yeah, I was shocked when she walked in, but I'm okay."

"I'm sorry if she upset you. You don't need that right now," he said as he took the washcloth and wet it once again. "I don't know how you could forgive her so easily."

"God commands us to forgive just as He forgives us," she said and took a breath to continue. She noticed Steve shake his head and roll his eyes. "What?" she asked.

"Nothing," he said as he twisted the water from the cloth and returned to her bedside, gently placing the rag on her forehead.

"No, what? When I mentioned God, you rolled your eyes."

"I just have a hard time believing this whole God stuff," he said as he sat in the chair.

"I know you've been hurt, but holding onto the anger of losing your parents is only hurting you. God loves you. No matter what happens in life, I know I'll be okay because God will help me through anything," she said as she snuggled further under the blanket.

"You sound like my granny," he said as a smile covered his face.

"Oh!" Darcy yelled as pain seared her tummy.

"What's wrong?" Steve asked, dropping the cloth into the sink as he returned to her side. Shock covered his face as he looked at the foot of her bed and noticed the bloody, wet covers below her waist. "Nurse!" he yelled. The nurse ran in, noticed the wet mess, and immediately left the room to get the doctor.

Within minutes, the doctor returned and started barking orders. He turned to Darcy and took her hand. "Darcy, your water broke. We have to take the baby."

"No, it's too early," she protested as her bed was being pushed from the room.

Steve stood frozen as he watched Darcy disappear down the hall, the doctor and several nurses in pursuit. Someone took him by the arm and led him to a waiting room. He sat dazed. He didn't even notice when his granny entered the room and sat beside him.

"Stevie, can I get you anything?" his granny asked as she placed her hand on his forearm.

Steve shook his head. "No, Granny. I'm okay. I'm just worried about Darcy and the baby."

"Honey, God will take care of her and the baby. Would you like to pray?"

He cut his eyes and glared at her. "Pray? Seriously?" he asked. "Granny, if God really cared, why did all this happen to her? To someone who believes in Him?"

"You were raised knowing Him, and you know man has free choice. You know bad things happen to His children because of their sin nature," she said, ignoring his scoff. "You are a child of His, Stevie, and you know He loves you. I understand you are hurt and never forgave Him for the murder of your parents," she said. The mention of his parents caused him to look at her. "You need to realize it wasn't God who killed your parents."

"I know He didn't kill them, but He allowed them to be killed while doing His work," he said, defending his anger and defiance.

"You need to let go of the anger and ask Him to forgive you, or it's going to destroy your life. Ever since their death, you have been angry with everyone. I know you can't be happy," she said as she patted his hand.

*Angry? Yeah, I'm angry. This anger got me through some tough situations in the Navy. My anger got me through, not God, h*e thought as she kept talking, her words lost on him.

She stopped talking as the doctor entered the room. He approached them. "Steve," he said. "Darcy's okay. She's in recovery."

"How's the baby?" Steve asked.

"The baby's in the NICU. He's in critical condition. He needs all the prayers he can get."

*He?* "When can I see Darcy?" he asked as he wringed his hands.

"She should be in a room in about an hour. I'll come get you when she's settled," the doctor said as he turned to leave.

Steve returned to his seat. A gentle hand touched his leg. "Let's pray for her, honey," his granny said in a voice barely above a whisper. Unable to think, all he could do was bow his head.

# EPILOGUE

*Four months later*

"Here they come," Hope said as everyone gathered in the living room. The room grew quiet as they heard the key enter the lock and the front door opened. "Welcome home!" the group yelled collectively.

Smiles covered Steve and Darcy's faces as they walked into the room full of loved ones. "Thank you so much," Darcy said, turning to Steve and taking the bundle from his arms. "Everybody, I want you to meet Christopher Seth Collins," she said as she uncovered her baby's face and tilted him so everyone could see the sleeping angel.

"Why don't you put him in the nursery," Steve said as he squeezed Darcy's shoulders. "Once he's in his crib, join us in the kitchen. I have a surprise for you."

Darcy grinned at him and turned and walked down the hall toward the nursery which they had worked hard preparing the last four months. Everyone else went to the kitchen, chatting away.

"Granny, thanks for not giving up on me. I don't know where I'd be today if I hadn't asked God to forgive me for my rebellion and anger. He's really been working in my life, and I can truly feel His presence," Steve said as he hugged his precious grandmother standing beside him.

"I love you, Stevie. I'm so proud of the man you've become," she said as she sat in the chair, which he pulled out for her at the kitchen table.

He sat beside her and noticed his sister across from them. "Cindy, thank you so much for putting all of this together. It's really nice."

She smiled and nodded. "You're welcome. I'm so happy the baby's okay," she said as everyone nodded in agreement.

"Yes, I'm grateful God protected him and has blessed all of us with the little guy," Steve said as Darcy entered the room. He stood and pulled out the chair at the head of the table for her to sit. Once she was settled, he began his speech. "I want to thank everyone for being here today. As you all know, it's been an exceedingly difficult few months for everyone but especially for Darcy. Before we partake of this wonderful meal prepared by my granny and sister, I'd like to give thanks," he said as everyone bowed their heads. "Lord, thank you for Your many blessings. Thank you for taking care of little Christopher and allowing him to be part of our lives. Lord, it's been a long four months, but we're grateful for Your mercy, forgiveness, and love. Bless each of us, Lord, as we seek Your will in our lives. Bless this food and the people around this table. Amen." Once he finished, everyone started passing bowl after bowl of food, and everyone filled their plates. Steve took time to help Hope who sat between him and Darcy. Dinner and chatter continued for over an hour. Once everyone had their fill, they gathered outside for cake and the revealing of the house Steve has worked so diligently on the last few months.

"Do you have the baby monitor?" Steve asked as Darcy took a seat on the bench beside the covered sign.

She smiled and held up the small box in her hand.

Cindy sat beside Darcy as Steve walked to the end of the table and began cutting the cake.

"Cindy, thank you for forgiving me for blaming you for Dillon's death. I'm really sorry for everything," Darcy said as she leaned toward Cindy and spoke so others couldn't hear her.

"It's okay. I really understand," she said as she placed her hand on Darcy's arm. "I'd probably feel the same way if I were in your shoes."

"Thank you for understanding. I can't imagine what you went through," Darcy said.

"You know, the hard part wasn't the physical abuse. The hard part was understanding God wouldn't want me treated like that. The hard part was letting go of Michael and depending on God. I don't know where I'd be today if my granny had not been persistent and loved me enough to keep talking to me about my relationship with God."

"Well, I'm glad you listened. I know it was tough on you when he was sentenced to life in prison, but I know God will take care of you."

"I'm sure He will. I meant to ask you, how did you come up with the name Christopher Seth?"

Darcy smiled. "Christopher was Dillon's first name, and Seth was my father's middle name."

"That's so precious," Cindy said as she looked up at the sound of Steve's voice.

"Can I have your attention for a moment?" he said as he tapped his glass with his fork. "Thank you again for joining us and celebrating such a wonderful occasion. We are so thankful to have little Christopher home and here to be a part of this blessed day," he continued as he motioned for Hope to join him. She immediately stood up and ran to his side. "All of you know Hope. She's a precious part of our lives and we are all happy she's here with us. You all know the situation which's brought her here. What some of you may not know is the wonderful thing that is happening because she's here," he said as he paused and picked her up. "See this beautiful girl is another reason we're gathered today." He smiled as he looked at her. She giggled as he bounced her in his arms. "Darcy, if you will, would you please pull the sheet from the sign when I nod?" he asked. Darcy rose and stepped beside the sign. "Life is tough, especially if you are alone. Hope was alone in this world since her parents have both gone to live with the Lord. That's until she was placed in our lives. Today, Darcy and I would like to share our dream and the next adventure in our lives," he said as he nodded. Darcy removed the sheet from the sign. Everyone gasped. "Everyone, help us celebrate the opening of *A Home for Hope.* We're going to open this home for children who need a loving home." Applause broke out. Everyone was talking as excitement filled the air.

Darcy heard Christopher over the baby monitor and headed into the house. When Steve noticed Darcy was in the house, he bent down and whispered into Hope's ear. She immediately ran into the house and returned moments later with a gift bag.

After a short time, Darcy returned to the celebration in the yard. She looked around at the people who were there to celebrate Christopher's homecoming and the opening of *A Home for Hope.*

*Lord, I am so blessed. Thank you for everything,* she prayed as tears filled her eyes.

"May I have your attention, one more time?" Steve asked. The crowd grew quiet once again. He grabbed Hope by the hand as they walked and stood beside Darcy. "So many of you have made this day so special for so many reasons. I'd like to thank Darcy for opening her home to me during a difficult time in my life," he said as he let go of Hope's hand and turned to face Darcy. "You are an amazing woman, Darcy, and I'm truly blessed to be part of your life," he said as she smiled at him. "I know you've been through a great deal and we've only known each other a short time, but will you do me the honor of becoming my wife?" he asked.

The only sound heard were birds chirping and the wind blowing. Darcy sat stunned, peering into his eyes. Slowly, she began to smile, and happy tears filled her eyes. "I know it's only been a few months since we've known each other, but it fills like a lifetime. We've been through so much together. Yes, Steve, I'd love to be your wife."

Hope squealed with happiness, and the crowd erupted in cheers as everyone started hugging the happy couple.

# ABOUT THE AUTHOR

Kim Sprayberry has survived a great deal in her short life. Having experienced abuse as a child and adult, she has much to share about life and reality with the readers. In her writings, she draws from her life experiences, intertwined with her vivid imagination, to tell a compelling story of abuse, similar to what she experienced. You will be captivated by her real Southern charm and ability to take you on a journey from Charleston, South Carolina, to Idaho in this gripping story of a family's devastation due to alcohol abuse. Kim's experience as a wife, mother, property manager, and expungement coordinator with the solicitor's office helping others in the criminal justice system get a fresh start shows her patience and empathy for others. Kim has a real passion for sharing through her writing and has written several articles and programs for her church and work. She also has experience directing plays and has a producer credit with the movie *I Hate Xmas*. She is married to her husband, Doug, for over twenty-five years with five children and three terrific grandsons. They live in the beautiful Greenville, South Carolina, area and love to travel while she embarks on her personal biography. Her desire to help others who have suffered abuse as a child or in a domestic situation is evident by her commitment to donate 100 percent of the profits from the sale of this book to charities who help people in those situations.

CPSIA information can be obtained
at www.ICGtesting.com
Printed in the USA
LVHW031057060821
693982LV00002B/10